AMANDA McKINNEY

Carol —
I hope you enjoy!

THE

WOODS

A BERRY SPRINGS NOVEL

Happy Reading,

Paperback ISBN
978-0-9989599-2-4

eBook ISBN
978-0-9989599-0-0
978-0-9989599-1-7

Credits
Editor: Teri Anne Conrad

Also by Amanda McKinney

LETHAL LEGACY

For my dad, who has supported and encouraged my love of writing since day one.

PROLOGUE

THE REFLECTION FROM the hot, summer sun blinded her as she stepped onto the white cliff. The heat radiated through the bottom of her boots and sweat began to bead on her forehead. Careful to not smear the makeup she'd talked herself into applying, she dabbed her face with the back of her hand.

Damn, Arkansas's summers were hot.

She glanced over her shoulder into the woods for what seemed like the tenth time.

What the hell was she doing? This was crazy. She was crazy. But, in all honesty, she'd done crazier things in her life. Hell, her life had been so chaotic lately, this little adventure seemed to fit right in.

It had been years and years of ups and downs—the ebb and flow of life her sister would call it. Years of not knowing what her future held and dealing with the restlessness that came along with that. Years of not planning or preparing enough to make her future a bright, prosperous one, and accepting a mundane existence as a result.

Jenna Somers was known for her spontaneity and her

'go with the flow' attitude. But, as she got older, that simple flow seemed to have quite a few more bumps in it.

It had been an unwavering cycle of constant chaos.

Chaos, chaos, chaos.

She knew she needed a change. She needed to do things differently. She needed to turn her life around. Maybe she'd start today.

She glanced at her watch. Five minutes late. What the hell?

A hot, humid breeze swept up her back as she stepped to the edge of the cliff. Bluebirds fluttered through the air a few feet from her face. The welcoming and familiar sound of nature filled her ears as she looked up at the sky, the cloudless, sapphire blue sky.

She smiled. It was her favorite spot. She'd been to the cliff a hundred times but was still awestruck at the picturesque view. There was the quietness—stillness—that only being this deep in the woods provided.

Atop the highest peak of Berry Springs's Summit Mountain, the massive rock sat high above a ravine that dropped down almost a thousand feet. A sparkling blue river cut through the bottom and on the other side was another steep, thickly wooded mountain. The beautiful Ozark Mountains.

It was postcard perfect.

She was lost in her own bliss when she suddenly heard leaves rustle behind her.

"Hey."

Nerves tickled her stomach as she turned to see him emerge from the tree line.

"Hi."

He looked nothing like she imagined. He sported a buzz cut that was thin enough to see his scarred, blotchy scalp. His features were sharp and defined. Despite the heat, he wore a red plaid shirt, tattered jeans and boots.

His eyes locked on hers and he slowly stepped onto the rock. She couldn't explain the sudden unease she felt.

Relax, it's just nerves, she thought as she glanced into the woods behind him.

A crooked smile cracked across his face as he said, "We finally meet."

She ignored the warning bells in her head and faked a smile. "Yes, finally."

He stepped closer. Almost instinctively, she scooted backward but stopped instantly when she realized her back was to the ravine.

Why the hell was she so jumpy? Why did this guy make her feel so... on edge?

She looked past him, into the woods, again.

A droplet of sweat rolled down the middle of her back.

He took a step closer.

Her pulse picked up.

"Beautiful day, want to sit down?"

"I... uh, I'm sorry, but I actually need to get back soon."

His face dropped and something sinister sparked in his eyes. "I just got here. Why so soon?"

"Well, you're late, and I... I've got a lot to do."

He narrowed his eyes and cocked his head, "Something wrong?"

"No, nothing..."

For a moment he stared at her, making her feel like she was stark raving naked in the middle of Times Square.

Creepy. This guy was totally creepy.

"I'm sorry, I need to go."

Get the hell out of here.

She took a step forward and he laid his hand on her arm.

Her stomach sank.

His dry pale lips narrowed and his voice lowered as he said, "What? Not impressed? I'm not good enough for you?"

Her eyes widened as she looked back at him. Evil. She saw the dark power of evil in his eyes as she snapped her arm away. "Get out of my way."

He raised his eyebrows and grabbed her wrist. "It's gonna be like that, huh?"

"Let me go."

His black, dilated eyes locked on hers.

That was the moment. The moment her sixth sense, her natural born instinct took over, and every inch of her body knew that that she was in danger. Real danger. She couldn't ignore it, couldn't close her eyes and wish it away. It was there screaming at her that her life was in stark danger.

Her heart hammered in her chest. She took one last look into the woods. Where the hell was her sister?

As she started to take a step back, his grip tightened. Her survival instinct kicked in and a rush of adrenaline suddenly burst through her veins.

"I said, *let go*." She raised her arms up to shove him backwards, but was blinded by a swift slap in the jaw. The metallic taste of blood seeped into her mouth as the pain vibrated through her head.

Fight.

Fight, Jenna.

She gritted her teeth and reared back to reciprocate the hit, but was too late. He shoved her backwards and her heels hit just a few inches from the edge of the cliff.

They say that most people instinctively know when they are about to die. They mentally retreat to a place that the living will never know about until the time comes for them.

That was Jenna's moment. That was the moment that she knew, without a doubt that she was about to die.

Blood dripped from her chin as she looked into his black eyes, which had gone from anger to wild, erratic. Bloodlust. His thin lips parted into a sneering smile as he reached down and grabbed the bulge in his jeans.

Her scream shattered the stillness of nature, moving through the wind like an animal being hunted.

"Shut up!" Charging her, he leapt forward.

Fight. Continue to fight. Fight until death.

As she crouched to leap forward, a gust of wind blew her off balance. Terror shot through her body as she shifted her weight.

Her heel slid off the edge.

The world around her seemed to stop as she began to fall backwards, her hands desperately grabbing at him. At *anything.*

For a brief moment, her fingertips caught his shirt and as if in slow motion, he slapped her hand away.

And then, as gravity pulled her body backwards, her last scream vibrated through the mountaintop as she tumbled off the cliff.

CHAPTER 1

"VINNIE! HAND ME my small trowel."

"Here you go, boss."

Holding her breath, Katie carefully wedged the tool into the moist, dense soil.

Although the cave was a cool sixty-two degrees, a thin layer of sweat coated her skin as she lightly pried the side of the object. No amount of deodorant could handle this kind of excitement, despite what the commercials say.

"Get me more light over here, Vinnie. And, Bobby, quit breathing down my damn neck."

Vinnie readjusted the flashlight as her team collectively took a step back. Katie never did like a crowd, and she wasn't shy about making it known.

"Come on," she whispered, before putting the tool in her mouth and pulling the brush from her belt. Holding her breath, she lightly swept away hundreds of years' worth of soil.

Had she really found something? Yes, yes, she had. She knew she had.

In a low, pleading voice, she coaxed the stone artifact. "Come on Miss Betty, come on."

She replaced the brush in her belt, pulled the trowel from her mouth and carefully began prying again.

The anticipation hung thickly in the air. Other than the *drip, drip, drip* of the stalactites, the cave was silent. Good. She'd trained her team well.

Pressing the small wedge just a hair deeper into the side of the cave, finally, she felt the mud give.

Whoosh!

The object released a suction-like sound as it loosened from the wall.

Katie dropped her tools, and with the utmost delicacy that only a woman could possess, she carefully removed the artifact.

Cheers erupted behind her and she couldn't help the small smile that spread over her lips.

"Okay, guys, back up. Let's get Miss Betty outside and into the light." She looked at the object and all but cooed. "You've been down here too long, haven't you?"

Behind her, she heard her partner, archeologist Bobby Zabel, chuckle as the team began to make their way through the narrow cave, careful not to touch anything they didn't have to.

Carrying the artifact like a newborn baby, Katie emerged from the hole in the ground to more cheers and questions.

"Dr. Somers, what is it?"

"Can we see?"

She shook her head. "Not yet." Always direct and to the point, she addressed the small crowd around the cave entrance. "Give me some time with her. We need to clean her up and take a look before I'll be able to tell you all anything."

Despite a few groans from the crowd, she briskly made her way into the tent and out of the scorching summer sun.

Katie and her team had been called to The Great Serpent Mound in southwest Ohio to explore a newly discovered cave underneath the snakelike mound. Being a beautiful and mysterious archeological site, Katie jumped at the opportunity to head up the excavation. And, thus far, the trip was proving to be worth it.

"Lay her here, doc."

She stepped into shaded tent, welcoming the cool breeze from one of the five box fans they had scattered throughout. Loose strands of hair from her messy ponytail danced across her face as she walked across the dirt.

While Bobby unloaded a case of tools, she placed the artifact on a folding table, pushed up her sleeves and slid on her glasses.

Shoulder to shoulder with her partner, they carefully began sweeping away the dirt, bat feces and sand from the small crevices on the stone tablet. Little by little, the intricate lines and curves carved on the surface began to come alive.

"See here," she pointed with her tool, "this looks like a plant. And this… looks like stars."

He nodded, "Some kind of celestial event."

"Exactly. And, these curves here…" she cocked her head, "A snake?"

"Possibly."

Bobby swept away more dirt from the bottom and a

small nested diamond design began to take shape. Unable to hide his excitement, he let out a boisterous *whoot whoot!*

Katie pulled out her magnifying glass and peered closer, and smiled. "Wow, yeah, I think that's the mark of the Adena culture. Nice work." She pulled a pen from behind her ear and leaned back, "So then, Betty's from somewhere between 1000 to 2000 BC"

She scribbled on a notepad as Bobby retrieved his camera from across the room.

She cocked her head, changing her view of the tablet. "A celestial phenomenon? An honor to a snake God, or Goddess?" Chewing her bottom lip, she took a moment to assess the artifact. "Let's get her completely cleaned up and then look at it with fresh eyes."

He nodded enthusiastically. "You got it doc, I'll take it from here."

One of Katie's mentors in college, Bobby was going on his thirty-second year of being an archeologist. And, although he was more than double Katie's age, he didn't bat an eye when she was given lead over the Serpent Mound project. Bobby was an archeologist because he loved the history, mystery and thrill of uncovering objects that shaped the very being of society. He did the job because he truly loved it, not for the fame or accolades. Bobby was a soft spoken, shy, work horse and he and Katie had formed a strong working relationship over the years.

Katie tore herself away from the tablet and glanced outside. "Okay. I'll go speak with the folks. And then we'll go back down in the cave… hopefully this isn't the only pretty lady we find; maybe Betty has a few friends."

"Fingers crossed, doc. Hey, are you sure you're stuck on Betty?"

Katie paused, and turned. "Yeah, why?"

Bobby shrugged. "Just curious."

As Katie started to turn, she paused, and then turned back around. "Wait a second, Betty was the name of your first wife, right?"

Bobby smiled, "Exactly. Never had too much luck with Betty."

Katie laughed. "Okay, we'll come up with a new name for her."

Years ago, when Katie was an intern, she'd began assigning names to each of the artifacts she found on her digs. She'd realized that it not only made recording and organizing more efficient, it also made each dig personal. And, each dig *was* personal to her.

Her job was her life. Archeology was her life. Ever since she was a little girl running around the rugged Ozark Mountains in northwest Arkansas, she'd collected and analyzed nature's gifts. Rocks, leaves, bird's nests, deer scat, you name it. But it wasn't until one rainy day that she'd picked up an archeology magazine at the local discount grocery store that she decided what she wanted to be when she grew up. An archeologist.

So, she'd set her sights on her goal and never looked back. And now, she was Doctor Somers. Doctor Katie Somers.

Katie was a born overachiever. Occasionally described as high-strung and uptight, she strongly believed that luck favored the prepared. So, she prepared for everything. Every single thing. If that made her high-strung and uptight, so be it.

After high school, she'd graduated Magma Cum Laude with a double degree in Anthropology and History. After that, she'd gone on to get her doctorate, graduating again, with honors. After college, she'd interned at several museums and agencies where she traveled the world until eventually finding a home with Samson Cultural Analysts. It was a prestigious agency that conducted archeological contract work all over the world.

Her current home address was a small New York City apartment, complete with one bedroom, one bathroom, a small kitchen and a postage stamp size balcony. The apartment had the bare essentials and scarce furniture, and her few friends told her that the place screamed bachelor pad... not bachelorette pad. Maybe so, but she traveled so much that it never occurred to her to decorate, or *feminize* the place as they'd suggested. She lived out of her suitcase and wouldn't have it any other way. Her career didn't allow for potted plants, seasonal flowers hanging in the windows, or men, for that matter.

Over the course of her career Katie gained national recognition for her publications on Native American culture. Requests to be a featured guest speaker at various events flowed in from all across the country, all year long. She was finally making a name for herself, and decent money at that.

Yes, her career was her life.

At thirty six years old, she had no husband, no kids, and no restrictions. And that was just fine with her. On the few lonely nights between jobs that she spent in her apartment with a glass of wine and tub of Ben and Jerry's, she would tell herself that she had her whole life to get married, have two point two children and paint a white picket fence. Although, she never was a fan of white, so maybe she'd go rogue and paint it brown.

Katie dusted the dirt off of her khaki tactical pants and made her way out of the tent.

"Miss Somers, congratulations. A tablet?" Dressed in a suit and tie, the Museum Curator stretched out his hand.

"Mr. Peterson," they shook hands, "thank you. Yes, a stone tablet from the Adena culture, I believe. This will be a great addition to the Adena Museum."

He nodded enthusiastically. "Yes, yes. What other markings are on it?"

"We're still cleaning her up and will do a thorough analysis after. You'll be the first to know."

"Do you think there's more?"

"I'm not one to assume anything, but my team will search again this afternoon."

"Great." He motioned to a media van parked off the mound. "The local news is here, we'd love for you to make a statement. Would you mind?"

She hesitated then shrugged. It wasn't the first time she'd been on TV covered head to toe in dirt. "Not at all."

After a brief press conference, Katie hiked back up the Great Serpent Mound to the tent.

"Your sister called." Bobby was hunched over a table, still cleaning the soon to be renamed Miss Betty.

Katie slapped her forehead, leaving dried dirt on her face. "Dammit, I was supposed to call her this morning." After wiping her hands on her shirt, he picked up her cell phone and dialed the number.

"Hey, Katie." A series of sniffles followed.

"Jenna, are you okay?" She closed her eyes shook her head, "I'm sorry, I mean, of course you aren't."

"Oh," *sniffle, sniffle,* "It's okay, I'm doing okay."

"It doesn't sound like it."

"Well, I'm just starting to unpack, and I… I just can't believe how my life has turned out. A divorce, moving out, *oh, Katie.*"

Katie squeezed her eyes shut. She never was the best at consoling her over-emotional sister, or anyone for that matter.

"Jenna, I'm sorry, but it's for the best, you know. The divorce, I mean."

Bobby quietly stepped over, showing Katie an email that needed her immediate attention. She shook her head and held up her index finger, one minute. "Um, you know, who needs a cheating bastard like that anyways, right?"

Heavy sobbing filled the cell phone.

Dammit. She hadn't heard her sister this upset in a long time. "Jenna, is mom there?"

"No, she went to the grocery store. But, you know her, crying never solves anything." More sobs.

"Okay," guilt panged her as she gripped the arrowhead necklace dangling around her neck, "Look, I've got a few days of free time after this project. Um, how about I come down and we can just hang out? Have fun. Do silly sister things."

Sniffle. "What? Really? You'd do that?"

She nodded, "Of course." From the corner of the room, Bobby dangled the phone toward her alerting her that she had a call. "So, it's settled then. I should finish up tomorrow and I'll book the next flight out."

"Here? *To Berry Springs?* My God, how long has it been since you've been here?"

Not nearly long enough, she thought but bit her tongue. "Almost ten years I think."

"Wow, the town will be shocked to see you."

Katie's stomach tickled with nerves. She loved her small hometown, but suffocating was a much better word to describe it. An extremely suffocating small town.

"Alright, Jenna I gotta go. Talk tomorrow."

"Okay, love you."

"Love you little sis."

"Hey, Katie?"

"Yeah?"

"It really means a lot that you'd come all this way just to cheer me up."

"Of course. We're sisters."

"Forever and ever."

"And ever."

CHAPTER 2

Welcome to Berry Springs
Population 1,326

KATIE'S FINGERTIPS DANCED on the steering wheel as anxiety began to brew in her system. Wow, it had been so long since she'd been back. She was just a teenager when she'd left for college and now she was all grown up; a woman. An independent woman with a life of her own. So much had changed.

Windows down, hair blowing in the wind, she inhaled the fresh, country air and a small smile spread over her face as she looked up at the sky. Bright colors of red, orange and yellow burst from the horizon where the sun had set just moments before. The large oak trees that she used to climb as a child danced in the warm summer breeze. Memories.

She reached over and picked up her phone.

"Katie!"

"Hey, Jenna."

"You made it?"

She released an exhale. "Yes, finally."

"I can't believe you didn't let me pick you up from the airport."

"Oh please, it's over two hours away, and it's nice to have my own car anyways." *For an immediate getaway, if a situation called for it.*

"Well, I wouldn't have minded. Anyways, you remember how to get here, right?"

Katie rolled her eyes. "It hasn't been *that* long, smartass. Should see you in less than thirty."

Her sister laughed. "Can't wait, drive safe."

Katie clicked off her cell phone, switched lanes, and drove onto the familiar bridge soaring over Queens River.

Berry Springs was a small, country town in the northwest corner of Arkansas, nestled in the Ozark Mountains. It was a beautiful area that experienced all four seasons to the extreme. Stifling heat in the summer, ice-cold in the winter, and picturesque spring and fall. It was a farmers' town, with all the country amenities you'd expect.

There was the town diner, Donny's Diner, adorned with red-checkered curtains that hung from the windows, where the gossip flowed like fresh coffee. The discount grocery store where long lines and screaming babies were inevitable. The farmers' market on the weekends; and the fast food place that became the local hangout after nine o'clock in the evening on weekends.

Big, loud trucks cruised the two-lane roads and American flags hung proudly from the town's square. Depending on the weather, it wasn't unusual to pass a family on horseback, going to and from their business.

Katie grew up hiking, fishing, camping and shooting BB guns. Although her dad took off when she was just four years old, her mother taught her and her sister how to be tough southern girls. Katie's mom, Bonnie Somers, was a fire-cracker, a no-nonsense kind of woman who was born and raised in Berry Springs.

Katie's sister Jenna was born three years after Katie and the two sisters couldn't be more opposite from one another. Jenna was a fly-by-the-seat-of-your-pants girl who never planned, committed to, or finished anything. A daredevil at heart, her decisions were made by what would give her the greatest rush. She'd barely made it out of high school, only to get married a few months later to the local rodeo star.

That marriage crashed and burned a year later, when Jenna woke up one morning and found a note from her husband, that said he was moving to Colorado to become a true rodeo star. Aside from settling the divorce, the two never spoke again.

Jenna then went on to marry the local liquor store owner, Zach, five years ago, and had recently learned that he had been unfaithful to her during their entire marriage. Their divorce was finalized last week and she had just moved back to their childhood home, prompting her current emotional breakdown.

Jenna had never lived anywhere other than Berry Springs, Arkansas, and probably never would.

Not only did they have different personalities, the two sisters looked completely different as well. Katie reflected their American Indian ancestry with long, straight, brown hair; big, sultry, almond-shaped eyes; and full, red lips. She was dubbed Poco in school, short for Pocahontas. She was lean and toned, which she attributed to marathon training and weekly hot yoga class—when she wasn't traveling and able to attend, of course.

Jenna, on the other hand, was a natural blonde, but bleached it a few shades lighter. She was three inches shorter than Katie and had a curvy, voluptuous body that men drooled over. Jenna seemed to find love easily, and was never short on boyfriends.

That was one of the few things that Katie was jealous of her sister, but it seemed that Katie spent more time worrying about her sister rather than looking for love.

Maybe it was because they grew up without a father, or because their mother worked days and nights, but Katie always felt a responsibility toward Jenna. To take care of her. It wasn't uncommon for Katie to handle everything from cooking dinner to helping with homework. Even all these years later, Katie felt like she needed to take care of her little sister.

Just like she was now.

It was seven-thirty in the evening when she finally crossed into the city limits. Memories flooded her as she drove by the small country club, surrounded by its less than impressive golf course. She smiled as she drove through the town square, and passed Donny's Diner.

She felt her cheeks flush as she passed the discount grocery store, the scene of her first kiss, with the grocery bagger aka football star. In the milk freezer, no less. It was a kiss she'd never forget.

So many memories.

Finally, she flicked the turn signal and made a left down County Road 26. Having had more than a few flat tires on the pothole-ridden dirt road, she took it nice and easy the next four miles.

Dense woods lined the narrow road and the familiar smell of pine perfumed the warm sunset breeze. She estimated that she had about thirty minutes of daylight left to help her sister unload as much as possible, once she arrived.

Her tiny rental car hit a pothole—bouncing her clear out of her seat—while turning left up the steep, winding rock driveway.

Anticipation filled her as the house she grew up in came into view.

She topped the hill and her mouth fell open as she laid eyes on it. It was everything she remembered, except it was extremely run down. In fact, the house looked like it was straight out of the last horror flick she saw in the movie theater.

She rolled to a stop behind the U-Haul van, turned off the engine, and stepped out of the car. The sound of heat bugs screamed in her ears as she put her hands on her hips and gazed up at the decrepit house.

Surrounded by thickly wooded forests, it was a small, one-story, rock house with a wraparound wooden porch and a porch swing. Behind the house stood the horse stable, which was already in bad shape the last time she visited, ten years ago. She remembered the house having character, old country charm. But not anymore.

From where she stood, she could see at least ten planks rotted out on the porch. The windows were dirty and cracked. The roof was missing shingles and the chimney looked tilted. How the hell does a stone chimney tilt? She raised her eyebrows and shook her head. Her sister had her work cut out for her, no doubt.

She grabbed her purse from the car, walked up the crooked steps and opened the thick wooden door. The smell of stale air and aged wood filled her nose as she stepped over the threshold.

Memories raced through her head and she closed her eyes for a moment and remembered what the house used to be—so warm and welcoming, with the smell of dinner in the oven, and the sound of wind chimes swinging on the back porch.

Mental note to get Jenna some chimes immediately, she thought.

"Katie!" Wearing a tank top, jean shorts and baseball cap, Jenna darted down the hall and threw her arms around her sister.

Katie closed her eyes, inhaling the sweet scent of her sister, who always smelled of vanilla. She pulled away and kissed the top of her head. It had been too long.

"How you doing, little sister?"

"Better now that you're here." Jenna glanced at Katie's neck. "Oh my God, I can't believe you still wear that thing."

Katie fingered the arrowhead necklace, "Hey, my little sister gave it to me, lay off."

"I gave that to you *decades* ago!"

She smirked, "Remember how mad mom was at us for going in that cave?"

"Yes," Jenna laughed.

Katie smiled and looked around the barren house. "Where the hell are all your boxes?"

"In the U-Haul out front. Some are already in the

rooms," she shrugged, "I really don't have that much, you know. Come on, set your purse down. I put some coffee on."

Katie flung her Louis Vuitton purse on the floor and took a moment to look around before following her sister. To the right of the entry was a large den with a stone chimney on the back wall. To the left was a small sitting area that their mother used to sew in. Ahead was a large kitchen with windows looking out to the woods.

The house had two bedrooms and two bathrooms. The master bedroom was large and boasted floor-to-ceiling windows that her mother saved for a year to have installed. The master bath centered around a claw-foot tub that Katie used to play in when she was little.

Everything was just as she remembered, yet so different at the same time.

Jenna met her in the hall and handed her a glass of iced coffee.

"So, mom hasn't really been keeping this place up, huh?"

Jenna shook her head, "Apparently not since she moved into her apartment years ago."

"You never came out here?"

She gave her sister a disgusted look, "Hell no, why would I?"

Katie laughed as they walked down the hall. Sweat began to slick her skin which reminded her of the one amenity the house did not have—central-air and heat. Even with all the windows open and fans blowing in every room, the house still felt like a sauna. "I forgot how damn hot it can get in the summer."

"I'm going to get a few AC window units tomorrow."

"Good." Katie took a sip of her coffee before saying, "Alright, let's do this."

"Do what?"

"Unpack your shit."

Jenna groaned.

"Hey, the sooner you get it done, the sooner this place will feel like home again."

"You're right, like always." She looked at Katie as tears filled her eyes. "I'm so glad you're here."

They spent the evening unpacking, organizing and gossiping—and sweating through the heat. Not surprisingly, Jenna felt the need to inform Katie of ten years' worth of Berry Springs gossip. Over the hours, Katie realized one thing to be true about small towns… not much changes. Certainly not in little, boring Berry Springs.

Mentally and physically exhausted, Katie tossed an empty box aside, sat back on her heels, wiped the sweat from her face and looked around at their progress. "Not bad." She glanced out the window. Somewhere between the gossip about affairs and firings, the summer sun had set and the blue glow of the moon began to shine through the trees.

"It's wine time."

A wicked grin crossed Jenna's lips, "Hell yeah. We've earned it. Let's go." She pushed off the floor and Katie followed her into the kitchen, which was more of a mess than the rotting porch outside. A box fat sat in the window, ushering the cooler evening air into the house.

"Ah, here we go." Jenna pulled two short wine glasses and a bottle of red out of a box.

Katie took a sip of wine and stood in the fans breeze. "It's cooler outside," she turned to her sister and raised her glass, "Wanna go outside?"

Jenna nodded, grabbed the bottle and stepped outside.

A million stars twinkled in the sky, dancing around the bright moon. The woods stood still and dark, flanking both sides of the house. Thankfully, the heavy humidity had subsided and the light breeze felt like silk across Katie's skin. She sat on the old porch swing as Jenna hopped up on the railing. Just like when they were kids.

"How's Greta?"

"She's good, Mom's got her over at Maddie's now. Maddie pretty much owns her at this point."

"I can't believe Maddie is still alive."

"And taking care of Greta. She still lives in the same house, just down the road."

"Mom should have just sold that horse."

"Yeah, but you know mom, she became emotionally attached."

"Well then why the hell did she decide to move to an apartment without finding a place for Greta first?"

Jenna laughed. "That's mom. I think she just got sick of this place." Her eyes lit up. "Oh, and we're all having dinner together tomorrow night. She's super excited."

"I talked to her on the way in, I'm excited to see her. Dinner here?"

"If I can get enough unpacked, yeah." Jenna looked down and took a deep breath. "Can you believe we're back here... I mean, *I'm* back here. Back in this house and out of a marriage. *Another* marriage." She bit her lip. "Jesus, Katie, my *second* marriage."

Katie heard the pain in her sister's voice and was suddenly so very glad she'd made the trip back to her hometown. "Things will get better Jen, I promise."

Jenna shook her head.

"Hey, at least Mom never sold this house; otherwise you'd be living in the woods."

"Very funny." The light from the kitchen window lit the look of despair on Jenna's face. "I just can't believe I have another failed marriage under my belt."

"He was a son-of-a-bitch for cheating on you Jenna, don't forget that. His fault. You don't need a man like that. No woman does. It's not your fault."

Jenna shook her head.

"It's *not* your fault."

Without responding, Jenna gazed up at the sky. A solid three minutes passed before she looked back at Katie. "Why haven't you ever married, Katie?"

Katie took a moment to respond and decided that the question called for honesty, not her usual witty response to avoid a deep conversation.

"Honestly, I don't know." Pause. "The one thing I do know is that the thought of marriage scares the hell out of me."

"It's because of Dad."

"What do you mean? We don't even know Dad."

Jenna laughed. "You really should go to counseling every once in a while."

Katie rolled her eyes.

"Seriously, it's because of Dad, but you and I just deal with it differently."

"Okay, go on Dr. Jenna."

"Well, look at me... I haven't been without a guy in my life since I was like fifteen years old."

With a wink, Katie said, "Yeah, you developed early."

Jenna grabbed her chest, "They are nice aren't they? No, seriously, I've been called promiscuous and probably worse things than that. You know that."

Katie clenched her jaw. She'd had to deal with the gossip regarding her sister her whole life, but that didn't mean it was okay.

Jenna shrugged, "And maybe that's true to an extent, but it's because I have zero respect for men. Because of Dad, because of him leaving us. To me, men are one hundred percent disposable. And then, there's you... You've never really had a serious relationship in your life. You're pushing forty and you've never been married and have no kids."

Katie dramatically clenched her heart, "Okay, shoot me now."

"I'm not insulting you, I'm proving a point. So, this is also because of Dad. You've never had a male figure in your life—ever—so you feel like you don't need one. Not only that, you don't trust men."

Katie suddenly felt like she had the weight of a hundred bricks on her chest. She opened her mouth to respond, but couldn't seem to gather her words. Feeling uncomfortable, she turned to her wit to avoid the subject, as she had done so many times.

"Geez, how many self-help books have you read lately?"

Jenna didn't laugh. She leaned her head back on the rail and took a deep breath, gazing up at the night sky.

Content with the silence, and letting the buzz from the wine sink in, they sat, watching the moon rise and the stars twinkle brighter.

Jenna eventually slid off the railing, gulped the last of her wine and said, "I'm beat. I'm going to bed." She walked over and kissed the top of Katie's forehead. "I love you, sister."

"I love you too, baby sister."

The screen door slapped shut as Jenna walked back into the house.

Katie poured another glass of wine and swayed back and forth on the porch swing. Just like she used to when she was a kid, sans wine, of course.

Her mind drifted to work and all the things she should be doing at that moment. But, here she was, back in Berry Springs, Arkansas. Back in the house she grew up in.

She started to put together a mental checklist of all the things they needed to do to the house, but her thoughts trailed to her sister, and how right she was on her assessment of their father and the effect him leaving had on them.

She was deep in thought when she suddenly heard something rustling in the distance. She sat up, the swing creaking in response, and looked toward the woods.

A feeling of unease crept up. One that she'd never felt at the house before.

Squinting, she leaned forward, and looked at the dark mass of woods.

Goosebumps broke out over her arms and she suddenly had the indescribable feeling that she was being watched.

It's probably just the wine, she thought but she couldn't shake the feeling.

While she scanned the vast area, she felt small and vulnerable on the porch. A sitting duck. The thick woods that surrounded the house were home to thousands of creatures—some little, and some big. Very big. With a thousand places to hide. What was out there, hiding, lurking in the shadows right now?

She sat motionless, straining to listen, hoping that her stillness blended her into the background.

And then, more rustling. Closer.

Her stomach dropped and she slowly glanced over her shoulder hoping Jenna was still in the kitchen. Nope.

She turned back and sat frozen, not moving a muscle.

A minute stretched by and the woods fell silent. In fact, the silence was deafening.

She sat still for a few more moments, then rolled her eyes and muttered, "God, toughen up Katie." After one more look into the woods, she pushed herself off the swing and walked into the house.

The door slammed shut behind her, the creaking porch swing slowly swaying in the breeze.

She clicked off the light, locked the door, and from deep within the mountain, the shrilling scream of a coyote pierced the silence.

CHAPTER 3

THE NEXT MORNING, Katie arose with the sun as she always does. She rolled over on the mattress on the floor, cursing at the crick that had formed in her neck overnight. With a soft groan, she sat up and turned off the box fan that was blowing directly into her face.

The early morning air smelled of fresh dew and wildflowers as it tickled across her nose. The humidity was low this time of morning, but definitely still there. Inhaling deeply, she stretched her arms above her head. She took a moment to listen and when she didn't hear anything, she assumed her sister was still asleep.

They had a lot to do, but the first order of business was coffee. With her hair bundled on top of her head in a messy bun and wearing nothing but a long T-shirt and panties, she padded across the house to the kitchen, carefully maneuvering between the stacked boxes. Dust sparkled in the streaks of sunlight beaming across the kitchen, reminding her that they needed to scrub every room from ceiling to floor. But first, coffee.

"Ha ha, *yes*," she said as she lucked out and found a coffee mug in an easily accessible box. It was the *"I Heart NY"* mug that she had gotten for her sister years ago. Although Katie didn't make it back home much, she always sent her sister little knickknacks and collectables from all the places she visited.

Not waiting for the brew to finish, she poured the steaming coffee into her cup and glanced out the window.

Dawn beckoned her and she stepped outside onto the porch. She closed her eyes, smiled and listened. Listened to the sound of the summer breeze blowing through the leaves in the tall trees; the familiar creaking of the front porch swing, and the gleeful chirping of birds. She could even hear the creek babbling in the distance. It stirred her soul and awoke something in her that had been tucked away for a while. But that warm feeling only lasted a minute.

She opened her eyes and her gaze landed on the woods, just past the field. She felt the same creepiness from the night before. She sipped her hot coffee but couldn't ignore the feeling of impending doom in her stomach. Why?

"Good morning sunshine."

She turned to see Jenna step onto the porch. "Good morning."

"The coffee woke me… it was nice to wake up to fresh coffee."

"No problem. How'd you sleep?"

"Like I was in a freaking sauna."

"Same here. We'll get some AC units when we go into town today."

Jenna hesitated, and glanced out to the woods. "I'm actually going to take Greta for a hike this morning, I think. We can go after that."

Katie cocked her head, surprised her sister would go for a hike when there was so much to do around the house. "A hike, today?"

"Yeah, I think so. Clear my head."

Her sister was avoiding eye contact. Something was up. "Well then, I'll go with you. Might be nice to get out in the woods again. Maddie has another horse doesn't she?"

"Uh, okay... yeah, she does. Harry."

"Harry the horse?"

They laughed.

"Alright, then. I'm going to check some emails and then shower."

"Sounds good." Jenna was busy scrolling through her phone. "I'm going to go shower now."

"Save me some hot water."

"Will do."

Katie watched as Jenna walked down the hall, her eyes never left her cell phone.

Two hours later, dressed in jeans, tank tops and cowboy hats, the sisters were horseback and on their way to the trail.

"The field has grown a lot."

"Yeah, I think I'm going to call Bud to cut it and sell the hay bales."

"Good idea."

The horses jumped over the wooden fence and stepped into the woods. Jenna glanced over her shoulder. "You remember the way?"

"To the cliff? You bet your ass I do."

As Jenna led and Katie trailed close behind, the horses took her time stepping through the thick brush. Katie looked around, nostalgia gripping her. Memories of her childhood flashed through her head. Chasing her sister on the trails, climbing trees, hopping fences, carving fake guns out of tree limbs, and playing cowgirls and robbers. Jenna was always the robber.

So carefree.

Katie watched the squirrels jump from branch to branch across the towering trees. Hummingbirds zipped past her, looking for fresh nectar. Needles from the pine trees crunched beneath the horses hooves. The woods were always so quiet and peaceful.

She took a deep breath and a small smile spread across her face. Lilacs. Brushing past her leg was an enormous lilac bush, in full bloom. The smell reminded her of her mother. She'd always have fresh lilacs in the house, during the summer.

"Jenna, look. Lilacs."

"Pick some, we'll put them in the house."

Gripping the saddle she reached down and popped off a branch. Harry, who apparently did not enjoy the slight slide of the saddle, kicked and nipped.

"Whoa boy, whoa." Katie stroked his neck. "It's okay, sorry about that." After sending her a menacing glare, Harry accepted the apology and went on about his business.

"Geez", she said under her breath as she gave Harry one last stroke before readjusting herself on the saddle. It had been years since she had ridden a horse, but it was just like riding a bike. A large, temperamental bike, with a nipping problem, that is.

Jenna laughed at Katie. "Need a riding lesson?"

"Oh shut up." Katie threw a branch at her sister.

"It's been too long, Katie."

"Oh, give me a break. I'm not used to Mr. Harry here."

"Yeah, yeah." Smirking, Jenna rolled her eyes and turned around.

After a steep climb, they finally broke through the brush and stepped onto a large rock that marked the cliff.

Taking in the view, Katie slid off of Harry and walked to the edge. "It's just as beautiful as I remember."

Jenna stepped up behind her. "I know, I still come up here a lot."

Katie took a deep breath and smiled as birds flew below her. The view was exquisite. She looked down. "The rivers up."

"Yeah, we had a lot of rain last week." Jenna glanced at her watch, "Hey... um..."

Katie shook her head from side to side, "Uh huh, we came all this way, don't rush me now. Hey, that cave is right around here isn't it?"

"Yeah, the opposite side that we came up."

"I want to go check it out, look for arrowheads."

"Always the archeologist."

"Wanna come?"

Jenna shook her head and glanced at her watch again. "Hang out with the bats? No thanks."

"You sure? What are you going to do?"

Jenna looked out toward the deep ravine. "Meditate, you know, work on my Zen."

Katie laughed. "Okay, I'll be back in twenty minutes, maybe less." She jumped on Harry. "I'll be right back."

"Love ya, sis."

Katie smiled as she slapped the reigns. "Love you too, see you in a sec."

Katie led Harry down the far side of the mountain. The cave was exactly where she remembered, and she mentally patted herself on the back for her sense of direction. She pulled Harry to a stop, slid off and tied him to a tree.

"I'll be right back buddy. Be good." She pulled a flashlight out of the saddle and stepped across the large rocks, slick with moss. The cool, moist air welcomed her as she stepped into the large opening of the cave. She loved caves.

A bat zipped past her head, sending a shot of fear up her back. "*Phew.*" She gave herself another mental pat on the back for not screaming. She'd been in a hundred caves, but never took to the bats.

She clicked on her flashlight and scanned the wet walls.

Growing up, she and her sister would come to the cave all the time. Jenna would write on the walls with rocks while Katie was busy digging up and analyzing anything that looked remotely interesting. She still had the three arrowheads that they had found together. One dangled from her neck.

As she stepped deeper into the cave, the *drip, drip, drip* of condensation echoed on the walls, like a ticking clock.

A clock counting down to something.

As she crept further, her sweat slicked skin cooled, almost to a chill.

With her flashlight in her hand, she crouched down and began sifting through the mud.

Drip, drip, drip.

Her senses peaked. Her breath went still as she raised her head.

Drip.

A distant scream vibrated through the air.

The hair on the back of her neck stood on its ends. She jumped up and sprinted outside. Hopping from rock to rock, she slipped, tumbling to the ground, busting her knee.

"Dammit!"

Another distant scream.

Her sister. It was her sister.

She scrambled off the rock, blood running down her leg, untied Harry and jumped into the saddle.

"Go, Harry!" She rammed her heels into his sides and he took off in a sprint back up the mountain. Branches ripped through her clothes as they raced through the woods.

What seemed like seconds later, Harry burst through the trees, landing on the cliff. Katie slid off the saddle. "Jenna?" Frantically, she looked around. "Jenna?"

Greta stood on the rock, snorting and slapping her hooves as if she understood the drama unfolding.

"Where is she, Greta?! *Where's Jenna?*" She yelled again. "Jenna!"

Greta stepped close to the edge and Katie's heart dropped. "No."

Holding her breath, she walked toward the edge of the cliff. A steep dip in the rock slanted downwards, to the very tip of the rock. Past that, was a thousand foot drop.

She got down on her hands and knees and crawled to

the edge. Her heart thrummed in her chest, panic buzzed in her ears.

She peered over.

At the bottom of the ravine, her sister's shattered body laid surrounded by a growing pool of blood.

"Jenna!"

Stars clouded her eyes and she had to keep herself from jumping down to her sister's body. She frantically looked around for a way down, but knew there was none.

"Jenna!" She hurled herself backwards, scrambling away from the edge.

The world spun around her. Faster and faster. A cold sweat broke out over her body as she doubled over and vomited on the rock.

"Oh my God, oh my God."

Feeling too dizzy to stand, she crawled over to Harry, pulled herself up and retrieved her cell phone. No reception.

She sank to the ground. The white rock felt like a frying pan and the sun felt like hot acid, burning her skin. Tears welled in her eyes.

Under her breath, she muttered, "I've got to call an ambulance. I've got to call the police." She started to stand when something caught her eye, reflecting in the sun.

She reached forward and plucked a small button off the rock.

CHAPTER 4

A year later...

KATIE GRIPPED THE steering wheel as she turned onto County Road 26. Her pulse picked up as her rental car bumped over the dirt road, taking her back in time.

She turned up the radio, attempting to calm the nerves dancing in her stomach. No luck.

It had been almost exactly a year since her sister's death, but it still seemed like yesterday.

After the funeral, Katie had left Arkansas and tried to resume normal life as much as possible. Work kept her mind busy during the day, but almost every night, her sister's scream vibrated through her ears, waking her from a deep sleep. The events of that day kept Katie up every night.

Although the Berry Springs Gazette ran the news with the headline, "*Hometown angel Jenna Somers slips and falls to her untimely death,*" something nagged at Katie that there was more to the story.

She had heard the scream. She had heard the second scream. The scream of fear. The scream of death.

Over the year, the town gossip ran rampant with conspiracy theories about Jenna's death. Although the police ruled it an accident, no one seemed to believe that she had just slipped and fallen. It didn't take but a few hours after the news broke for all eyes to be on Zach, Jenna's cheating ex-husband.

But, Zach not only had a handful of alibis for the hour that Jenna died, he was also on camera entering the building where he worked and not leaving again until after five o'clock in the evening. Rumor had it that Jenna's death and the gossip that came with it turned him into a hermit, who rarely left his house so he didn't have to face the accusatory glances.

Unable to bare the loss of a daughter, Katie's mother had booked a one-way ticket to England to spend time with distant relatives. The last time Katie spoke with her, she had no intention of returning any time soon, and would appreciate if Katie would handle the selling of their family home.

So, here she was. A year later, driving her rental car down the dirt road that led to their childhood home that she was going to put up to sell. The last home Jenna had ever lived in.

Katie veered left and drove up the steep driveway. Even in the bright summer sun, the house looked cold and dark.

She rolled to a stop and turned off the engine. Every muscle in her body tensed and she felt frozen in the seat of her car.

As she gazed at the house through the windshield,

she took two deep breaths and said, "You can do this." *Be strong, Katie.* She made a promise to herself that she would *not* fall apart. Not now.

She set her jaw, unbuckled her seatbelt and got out of the car.

The familiar sound of the surrounding woods filled her ears, the summer bugs humming as she walked up the steps and unlocked the front door.

The stale heat suffocated her as she looked around.

Everything was exactly as she and Jenna had left it when they went out for the hike.

She let out an exhale and went through each room, opening the windows and turning on the fans.

First order of business, get everything packed up and organized. Katie and her mother had decided to donate everything of Jenna's to the local thrift store. That's what she would've wanted.

She estimated that would take a full day, maybe two. After that, she would spend a day doing the best she could to fix up the place. Fix the small things like the loose cabinet handles, squeaky doors, rusted spouts, and maybe replace a few rotted planks on the front porch. Then, she'd tackle the nicks on the walls with touch up paint and maybe slap a new coat of primer on the back porch. Last, but certainly not least, she'd clean the house from top to bottom. That was the job she dreaded the most. Then she'd meet with the realtor, sign all the necessary paperwork, and leave it to them to sell the damn thing.

If luck was on her side, she'd be back on a plane to New York by the end of the week.

She retrieved her luggage from the car, dragged it to

the bedroom and changed into a tank top and jean shorts. She wrapped her hair in a bun, slapped on a red bandana and contemplated what room to hit first.

She glanced down the hall to her sister's room.

Do not fall apart.

Despite reminding herself to be strong, she felt the sting of tears and decided she'd save that room for last and made her way into the den.

Only a few boxes filled with books and pictures were scattered on the hardwood floor. Candles and knickknacks were placed on the fireplace mantel—exactly where she had unpacked them with her sister a year ago.

She put on her earphones, cranked some classic rock, knelt down and began organizing each box. The hours flew by as she kept her head down and mind busy.

Just get it done, she kept telling herself.

Halfway through the fourth box, she noticed something sparkling underneath some picture frames.

A small ring, with three small diamonds on the band. Jenna's ring. She'd seen her wear it often growing up. Smiling, she slipped it on her finger. Perfect fit.

Her eyes filled with tears. Frustrated with herself, she pulled off her earphones and took a deep breath. She needed a break.

She found the remote and clicked on the television. As the local news drowned out the silence, she was grateful she had the foresight to call ahead and have all the utilities turned on prior to her arrival.

A red banner with the word "ALERT" ran across the top of the screen. She turned up the volume.

"... *received word of a credible threat. As you can see*

behind me, the Capitol building has been evacuated while the SWAT team searches room to room. New information is trickling in by the minute here, and I'll keep you updated. Reporting live from Arkansas, this is Amy Duncan. Back to you at the station."

She sat back on her heels. A threat at the Capitol building? Nothing like that ever happens around here. The worst thing she remembered growing up was when the McKinney boys accidently set fire to the local fireworks stand, which coincidentally set fire to a few of the surrounding buildings. At least, they said it was an accident.

She glanced out the open window where dusk's dark shadows cascaded over the yard. She'd been hard at it all day and realized that she was completely exhausted. Physically and emotionally. And starving.

She pushed off the floor and padded to the kitchen, which was left in the same scarce shape as it had been a year ago. She might have had the foresight to turn on the utilities, but not to get food in the house.

Already knowing what the outcome would be, she opened the refrigerator door and gazed inside. An old Arm and Hammer baking soda box, empty jar of jelly and a bag of coffee. Nice.

There was always fast food, but the last thing she wanted was to run into someone she knew and get pelted with questions and sympathy. Although it had been a year since the death of her sister, she knew people would still talk about it. Especially, in this small town.

"Dammit." She slammed the refrigerator shut. Any food was better than no food.

She grabbed her keys, slipped into her flip flops and jumped in her rental car.

Thirty minutes later she drove down Main Street, the narrow two-lane road that cut through the center of town. It was a quiet Monday evening and she'd only passed a few cars on the road, which didn't surprise her considering the entire town shut down at nine o'clock.

"Where to go… where to go…" She tapped the steering wheel and looked around.

Gino's Pizza.

The decision was made by her stomach growling on cue after seeing the sign. She whipped into a parking spot, glanced at her reflection in the mirror, and then made her way inside the Italian eatery.

Gino's Pizza had opened a few years ago in hopes of breaking the curse of the building, which every restaurant that opened under its roof shut down within twenty-four months. When Katie was in high school, it was a popular hamburger joint, then a bar, and then another burger joint.

The restaurant still had the same worn hardwood floors, cracked walls, high beam ceilings and old-school juke box sitting in the corner.

The smell of warm dough, cheese and beer perfumed the air. It was heaven. Her mouth began to water as she took a seat at the bar.

"What can I get ya, ma'am?" The young, freckle-faced waiter wiped his hands on a towel.

"One slice… wait, two slices of triple meat, please."

"Anything to drink?"

She hesitated, then thought *what the hell*. "A beer."

"You got it." He filled a pint glass and slid it down the bar.

She took a deep gulp when her attention was drawn to two burly men in cowboy hats discussing something on the television. The local news was running the same story she had been watching at the house. Big news, apparently.

"Damn terrorists."

The other man stuffed a rolled slice of pizza in his mouth. "They'll attack anywhere. Hell, here? I mean, what the hell is in Arkansas?"

The bigger man puffed out his chest. "What's here? Well, I'll tell ya what's here, two sawed off shot guns if they ever make their way into my backyard."

The other man nodded and tapped his companions drink before swigging the remaining contents of his own.

"Here you go, ma'am." She couldn't help but smile at her waiter calling her ma'am. Was she really that old? No. No, that was just one of the many characteristics that separate true Southerners from the rest of the country. No matter how old, or how young, in Berry Springs, Arkansas, kids were taught to address others by ma'am and sir.

"Thank you, sir." She smiled.

Her stomach audibly growled as she looked down at the grease covered slices on the red and white checkered plate. This was officially the best part of her day. Her mouth watered as she picked up the first slice, rolled the corners and began to raise it to her mouth. Before she could take a bite, she heard a familiar voice.

"Poco!"

She turned and saw her high school friend, Greg. Dammit, she was so close to getting out of there without having to relive the past.

"Greg." Smiling, she slid out of her chair and walked into his open arms. *Here we go*, she thought as they embraced.

"Little Miss Katie Somers." Another one of her classmates stepped up.

She released Greg and smiled, "Paul. Wow," she looked back and forth between the two, "it's been so long since I've seen you both."

With red hair and freckled skin, Greg looked like the poster child for an Irish commercial. He was adopted as a child and transported to Berry Springs in the eighth grade and never quite fit in. Having had a soft spot for kids who struggled socially, Katie had made an effort to befriend him while most others seemed to ignore the "new kid."

Paul was a few years younger than Katie and shared a class with her sister, Jenna. He was the quarterback of the football team, homecoming king, the list went on and on. Being the most popular guy in her grade, Jenna had dated him off and on for years.

Greg put his hand on her shoulder, "Hey, I never got to tell you, I'm so sorry about your sister. How ya doing?"

She looked down. "Thanks. Okay, I guess."

Paul slid his hands in his pockets. "I'm sorry too. I was at the funeral."

"Oh, I didn't see you, I'm sorry. That day was so…" she closed her eyes and shook her head.

"I know. I know it was. It was hard for everyone."

A moment of silence ticked by.

"What are you doing back in town?"

The dreaded question. "Well, we need to sell the house, so... so, I'm here to get that done." She slid back onto the barstool.

"The house you grew up in?"

She nodded.

"Wow, you guys have had that house forever, right?"

Another nod.

"Well, if you need help with anything, you can give us a call."

"Thanks." Time to change the subject. "How are you guys? Gosh, how long has it been since I've seen you?"

Greg took a seat next to her. "Awhile."

The waiter slid two coasters across the bar. "What can I get you guys?"

"Two beers." Greg smiled and turned back to Katie. "You look great. I hear you're some big shot doctor these days."

She laughed. "Hardly a big shot—I'm not saving lives or anything. Just an archeologist."

Paul sipped his beer and wiped the froth from his lips. "Yes, you are a big shot. I read some of your articles. Impressive." He glanced down at her finger. "So, no lucky man or anything, huh?"

She took a bite of pizza and shook her head, "Nope."

"Well I'm sure all the boys will be after you while you're here."

The front door dinged, followed by a loud gasp. "Katie!"

Her old friend, Brit, ran across the room. Before Katie could stand, Brit wrapped her arms around her, sloshing Katie's beer in the process, covering half her uneaten slice of pizza. "Oh my God, Katie! Girl, what are you doing here?"

Growing up, Brit and Katie were always friendly but didn't have the same circle of friends. Brit was a true Southern cowgirl, a proud member of the FFA and crowned winner of Miss Hog, not once, but two years in a row. A walking stereotype, she had bleach blonde hair—always hot rolled—accentuated by bright red lipstick and cowboy boots to match. Never a wallflower, she was the type of gal to always keep the conversation rolling and was the life of the party. She would give you the shirt off her back if you needed... or, after a few shots of good 'ole Tennessee whiskey, maybe you wouldn't even have to ask.

Greg cut in before Katie could answer. "She's getting the house ready to sell."

Brit dramatically inhaled, "Are you serious? Your childhood home?" Then, apparently remembering the events of last year, her face dropped, "Oh, Katie I'm so sorry. I forgot for a minute. I'm sorry. That must be so hard for you."

"It's fine, it's okay."

"How long are you in town for?"

"Just as long as it takes to get everything done."

Brows furrowed with concern, Brit put her hand on Katie's back. "Did any new information ever come out?"

Katie's stomach dropped and a knot began to form in her throat. "No. No, just that she must've got too close to the edge... and fell."

Greg gulped his beer. "Bullshit. How many times had you guys been to the cliff?"

"More than I can count."

"Exactly. I'm sorry but it just seems pretty coincidental that right after she found out Zach was cheating on her and pulled the plug on her marriage, she... ya know."

Katie clenched her beer tighter. "He had multiple alibis for that day. He was at work. And anyway, I hear that he pretty much doesn't even come out of his house anymore except to go to work."

Greg leaned back in his chair. "Well shit, I'd stay behind closed doors if everyone was constantly giving me the side eye, knowing I murdered my ex-wife."

Brit cocked her head. "Knowing? He had, like, ten alibis Greg. Lay off. The dude's been through enough."

Katie put her hand over her churning stomach. She needed to get the hell out of there. She flagged down the waiter. "Check, and box, please?"

"Oh, we didn't mean to run you off." Greg grabbed her arm.

Paul shook his head, "Dammit, guys. Way to ruin her night."

"No, it's okay, I really need to get back. There's so much to do."

"I'm sorry, we shouldn't have even brought it up."

"It's alright, really. I just need to get going."

"Okay, well call me if you need anything."

Brit stepped in for a hug. "This must be so hard for you. Let me take you out for a drink while you're here, okay?"

Katie smiled, "We'll see." She signed the bill and boxed up the remaining slice of pizza. "See ya guys."

She was tense, agitated the whole drive home. The conversation brought up old memories, old conspiracy theories. She'd expected it, really, but it didn't make it any easier. No wonder why her mom skipped down.

She pulled up the driveway. The darkness of night

coated the house and she kicked herself for not thinking of turning on a light before she left.

The front door creaked as she pushed it open and stepped inside. The house was silent. Eerily silent. She gripped her purse like a weapon, flicked on the entry light and looked around. Everything was just as she'd left it.

"Oh, stop it," she muttered to herself as she flung her purse on the floor, walked to the kitchen and turned on the window fan.

In a foul mood now, she reached for the wine and leaned against the counter. The sound of the whining fan buzzed in her ears as she glanced out the window and gazed into the black woods.

She took a sip of wine, scanning the tree line.

Nerves tickled her stomach. When the hell did this place get so creepy in the nighttime?

"*Dammit, Katie.*" Pissed off at herself for being scared, she clenched her jaw. What the hell was wrong with her?

She was no wimp. And she wasn't going to let her frazzled emotions get the best of her. Instead of turning away from the window, she squared her shoulders and walked right up to it and looked out.

The world was still except for the porch swing that drifted back and forth in the evening breeze.

CHAPTER 5

HANDS TREMBLING, HE veered left on the dirt road—or, what was left of it—and her red sports car came into view. His headlights cut through the darkness, illuminating her small frame in the driver's seat. He slowly pulled up next to her and rolled down his window, as she did the same.

With a blank expression, she stared straight ahead. His heart began to beat faster. Was she still pissed? Was it over? It had been two days since he'd seen her. Two days too long.

"Baby, come here."

She narrowed his eyes and looked at him. "Your crazy wife isn't right behind you, is she?"

Yep, she was still pissed.

He shook his head.

She rolled her eyes, pushed out of her car, sauntered around the back of his truck and jumped in the passenger seat.

Her attitude was as thick as her discount dollar store perfume.

He leaned forward. "I'm so sorry. I didn't know she followed me that night."

She made a *tsk-tsk* sound and shook her head, her perfectly curled hair bouncing on her pointy shoulders. "You know, I've got enough stress in my life, I don't need that, too."

He put his hand on her leg, "I know, baby, it won't happen again, I promise."

"I bet the whole freakin' town knows now."

His stomach knotted. He had no doubt the gossip was spreading—and quickly.

She continued, "I mean, what's this going to do to my career, Carl?"

He shook his head. "Nothing. If anything, it will just make you more popular. Look, I'll keep giving you exclusives and you'll be good."

She rolled her eyes.

"You're already becoming a reputable journalist with all the secrets I spill to you, you know."

Annoyed, she raised her eyebrows. "Well, I don't need this shit with your wife right now, Carl, it could wreck everything for me."

He wanted to get the hell off this conversation and down to business. He scooted closer. "Everything's going to be alright, okay?" He tickled her ear. She always loved it when he did that.

A small smile spread across her red lips. Those lips. He knew exactly what she could do with those full, thick, red lips. His skin tingled with excitement just looking at her face. How did he get so lucky? She was the sexiest woman in the county, and she slept with him. With *him*.

Deep down, he knew that she just wanted information from him, a cop with all the local dirt. But, it was worth it for just five minutes with her. He gave her what she wanted, and she gave him what he wanted. Even, if it was wrong.

Damn her and her power over him.

He glanced in his rearview mirror to confirm they were still alone. The spot—*their spot*—was just off of a secluded one-lane dirt road on the way out of town. The small clearing made by hunters was just big enough to fit both of their cars, and was completely surrounded by thick trees and brush.

He turned off his truck and the sound of a million bugs screamed in the humid evening air.

She turned toward him and with a pout said, "Are we done? Over?"

He took a moment to respond. "No."

She slowly scooted across the long seat and nuzzled up to him. "Good."

He looked over at her, her face lit by the moonlight spilling in through the windshield. "I would never be done with you."

Something sparked in her eyes. She removed her suit jacket and turned her body toward him, pressing her voluptuous breasts against the side of his arm. Her low-cut tank top left little to the imagination. She leaned forward, his arm practically in between her breasts now, and rubbed her lips against his ear. In a low, deep whisper, she said, "I've missed you the last few days."

His pulse picked up as he felt her hot, moist breath on his skin.

She flicked her tongue against his earlobe. God, the things she could do with that tongue.

He looked at the blue glow of the radio clock. "I have to get back soon."

She smiled, as if accepting the challenge. "It doesn't have to take long." She grabbed his chin, turned his face to hers and crushed her lips into his. Her tongue slid into his mouth as she tightened her grip on his chin. She was in control—she knew it, and he knew it.

He melted into her mouth, into the seat. As if sensing his surrender, she slowly trailed her hand across his leg and onto the bulge beginning to grow in his pants.

Goosebumps broke out over his body as she lightly gripped him. A rush of blood between his legs stiffened him like a rock. He groaned as she rubbed him through his pants while her tongue caressed his neck.

Eyes wide, heart pounding, he watched while she pulled the tight tank top over her head. Her breasts spilled over her black lace bra, which she undid while her eyes locked on his. The smell of her perfume filled the cab of the truck. Peonies, she smelled like fresh peonies. And hot sex.

His hands began to tremble, and his heartbeat pulsed between his legs.

She smiled that smile.

Wild with lust now, he pushed himself away from the steering wheel, angling himself over her as she leaned back. He guided the back of her head against the passenger side door, pulled her skirt up around her waist and hastily yanked down her silk panties, popping the tiny side strand in the process. With his left hand he grabbed her breast, squeezed. Squeezed so hard, he didn't know how she could stand it, but she did. She loved did.

He was panting now, heavy. While his hand was busy on her breast, he trailed his other finger down past her belly button, down a little further and then to her soft pad of hair. He felt the animalistic heat radiating from between her legs and his mouth filled with saliva.

He knew what she wanted.

Without preamble, he slid in a finger, feeling the slick wetness gather underneath his fingernail. She released a groan in appreciation as his finger slid back and forth, back and forth. Again, and again. Her breathing picked up, inhaling through her nose, exhaling loudly.

He loved to hear her pant.

With his hands busy he looked at her beautiful face, her lush lips parted slightly, allowing the soft groans to escape from her throat as he worked his fingers. He wished he could take a picture and look at it forever.

Even wetter now, she arched her back, her hard nipples pointing to the sky. She was almost there. The moonlight illuminated the sweat sheen on her perfect body.

She was an angel, his angel.

He slid his fingers in and out of her wetness, while rubbing her clitoris with his thumb. He watched her jaw clench in pleasure as he inserted another finger. In, out. He rubbed her harder, faster. She gripped the side of the seat, opened her mouth and with a scream he felt her body pulsate with a rush of liquid.

After she finished, he pulled away, pushed himself up and with trembling hands, released his belt, unbuttoned his pants and slid out of his boxer shorts.

He was throbbing, tingling and frantic.

Damn, he hated that she could do this to him.

With lazy, worn eyes, she smiled again. Yes, she knew what she did to him.

He placed himself over her, picking her head up and resting it on his forearm. One leg on the seat, one leg balancing on the floorboard, he lowered himself and plunged his rock hard cock into her wetness. Her fingernails stung into his back as he thrust himself in.

"Oh baby." He slid out, savoring the sensation, then plunged in again. And, again.

"Fuck me, baby."

Harder. Again, again, in, out.

"Say my name."

"Oh, Amy." His voice trembled. "Amy."

Sweat dripped off his forehead and onto her face. Chill bumps ran over his skin, spots sparkled in his eyes.

She breathed, "Oh, *Carl.*"

His whole body tensed, trembled. With a final thrust, he exploded himself into her.

She flashed him a smile, and a wink, as she reversed her sports car and pulled onto the road.

The cab of his truck smelled like sex. Sweat and sex.

Composing himself, he leaned his head back on the headrest and took a few deep breaths. It—*she*—really was like an addiction. He thought about her all day; about her face, her lips, her breasts, her wetness. And then he would get it, and it would somehow be even better than the time before, every time.

He looked down and rolled his wedding ring around his finger. It was her fault, his *wife's* fault. At least that's what he would tell himself after banging the local news anchor.

He and his wife had been high school sweethearts and married right after graduation. Her parents hated him and he couldn't have cared less. He was in love with Suzie— head over heels in love. It wasn't long into their marriage that Suzie got pregnant and they started a family.

Things went well the first few years—Carl got a job at the police station and Suzie became a school teacher. But, as the years went on, their marriage went on autopilot. Every day was the same routine. Get up, feed the kids, get to school, go to work, come home, eat dinner, get the kids to bed, go to bed.

They quit having sex. On the rare occasion that they did, it was boring, to say the least. She stopped having orgasms. He could usually bang one out, but only while fantasizing about the actress on the television in the background.

He gained weight, started losing his hair, then lost all of his self-confidence and self-worth. He started volunteering to work the graveyard shift, just so he wouldn't have to pretend to be happy at home.

He should have seen it coming, really.

She started having "meetings" after school, became even more distant, began getting late night phone calls, and the list went on.

Then sure enough, one evening he finally got the balls

to go through her phone and there it was. Sexual text messages between his wife and the Jr. High basketball coach.

She was cheating on him.

He yelled at her, she cried, said she was sorry and that she would break it off. This went on for years. But he could never bring himself to leave her. That was the funny thing. No matter how many men she had sex with, he still loved her.

Years and years this went on. She cheated on him, and he stayed faithful to her.

But, something about her most recent affair sent him over the edge, and looking at himself in the mirror one day, he made a decision. If she was going to do it, he would too. So, he pursued little Miss Amy at NAR News, enticing her with exclusive details on local stories. It was easier than he thought it would be. *She* was easier than he thought she'd be.

The first time was one of the most nerve racking experiences of his life. What an adrenaline rush! He was doing something bad, but something so exciting at the same time. Better than that, he was getting back at his cheating wife. Finally, he wasn't the only one with a dirty little secret in their marriage.

But best of all, he was getting off regularly.

That all started six months ago, and he was now having more sex than he ever had in his whole life.

So, why the hell did he feel so empty afterward?

CHAPTER 6

AFTER POURING HIMSELF a cup of coffee, Jake stepped onto the deck to find his mother sitting in her favorite rocking chair, sipping her morning coffee. Always get up before the sun, she would tell him.

"Morning, Mom."

A smile as wide as the horizon spread across her sleepy face. "My beautiful, perfect son. Good morning." Curled at her feet, her one hundred and ten pound German Shephard, Shotsky, opened one eye and snorted at Jake.

He bent down and ruffled the dog's ears. "Morning, buddy."

"Did you sleep alright?"

Jake stood, and in nothing but a faded pair of jeans, he leaned against the porch railing and sipped his coffee. "I did. It's nice here."

"It sure is, I'll get your room organized today. It'll feel more like home."

Jake looked beyond the pastures, out to the mountains. The morning sun was just beginning to break through and a rainbow of colors illuminated the sky. The surrounding woods sang with chirping birds looking for their morning breakfast, and in the distance he could see the outline of a deer and her fawn. It really was beautiful, although nothing like their hometown in Montana. For a moment, his stomach clenched, hoping that his mom would find contentment and happiness at this new house.

"Don't trouble yourself Mom, my room's just fine."

"It's no trouble at all, son."

Jake learned at a young age not to argue with his mom, so he bit his tongue and changed the subject. "It's a beautiful house. Fits you."

She smiled and leaned her head back against the chair. It did fit her, and she was glad she made the difficult decision to move.

Not long after Jake's father died, his mother, Nora, decided to sell the family home and move south—to a small town that his grandmother grew up in. Berry Springs, Arkansas. The town was starkly different from his hometown and he was surprised by her decision, but whatever made her happy.

After making a considerable profit selling the Montana mansion, Nora purchased a newly renovated rock and log estate on almost three hundred acres that included lush pastures, steep mountains with hiking trails and a river front. It was her first week in the new house, and he still wasn't sure who she planned to take care of everything, but he had no doubt that his mother would rope in some gullible cowboy within a few days to take care of the house and land.

She looked up at him, smiling. "I just can't believe you're here. It makes me so happy."

"Temporarily, remember."

"I know, I know. I'll take what I can get." Her face pulled tight with concern. "How's your back?"

"It's fine Mom, don't worry about it."

"It's a mother's job to worry."

"Well, I'm a grown man now. You need to worry less… it's not good for you to worry."

"Oh, you'll always be my baby. One day you'll understand."

Jake hated making his mother worry, and he'd sure done a good job of it since he joined the Army straight out of high school. Being the only man in her life now that his father had passed made things more complicated. He found himself worrying about her constantly. About her health, her security, her happiness.

"So, what's on the checklist today?"

Contemplating, she took a sip of coffee and then said, "Well, thanks to all your help, we've gotten most of the unpacking done. Not too much left to do. You were right about downsizing. And I love this area… your grandma was right about it here."

"We just need to get you some friends and you'll be all set."

"I've yet to visit the local beauty salon, which is where I'm hoping to hear some gossip and meet a few folks. And…" A smirk spread across her face, "My horses should get here today."

Jake lowered his coffee and raised his eyebrows. "Horses? Our horses?"

"Yep. My life isn't complete without my horses, you know."

Exhaling, he dropped his shoulders. "Mom, I thought

you were going to sell them. Horses take a lot of work. Work that Dad took care of."

Nora took a deep breath. "I know, but they remind me too much of your father. I can't part with them. And besides, Butch just finished his last round of training. He should officially be smarter than me now." She bent over and stroked Shotsky. "But not as smart as Shots here."

"No one's smarter than you, ma." He winked. "How are the horses getting here?"

She grinned. "Well, I couldn't part with the family plane either."

He shook his head. "You also told me you were selling that damn thing." He sighed. "Where do you plan on keeping it?"

"There's a small hanger not far from here."

Jake shook his head, again. "Just wait till the locals find out you have a plane, Mom."

She laughed, "I'll be the most popular kid in school."

Jake smiled and scanned the nearby fences. "I'll need to make sure the fences are secure for the horses, then."

"Yes, thank you dear."

They both sat in silence for a moment, watching the sun rise and listening to the sounds of the country. Finally, his mother addressed the elephant in the room.

"How long will you be here?"

Jake looked down. Guilt fluttered in his stomach. "I'm not sure."

"So, they just want to make sure your back is healed completely? Right?"

He paused. "Yeah, I guess so."

She narrowed her eyes, "So, the Army is just giving you a bit of time off, then? Official leave?"

Avoiding eye contact, Jake simply nodded while gazing at the rising sun.

She reached over and put her hand on his arm. "Why don't you tell me more about what happened… other than getting blown up by an IED?"

Jake took a long sip of his coffee. "That's about it. Please, don't worry about me."

She sighed and leaned her head back on the rocking chair. "Like I said, it's my job."

Born and raised in a small town in northern Montana, Jake Thomas was born into a hard-working, wealthy family, rich in legacy. His grandfather was a miner who, along with several of his colleagues, invested in a small oil company that eventually became Montana's main source for petroleum. But, always an instinctive business man—and much to the surprise of his colleagues—he sold his stock at the height of the boom. The move paid off for Herbert Thomas. Shortly after his exit, the company went under, unable to compete with the growing oil conglomerates, leaving nothing but debt in its dust.

Herbert and his three sons invested wisely and more than quadrupled their net worth over the next few decades. To their fathers urging, each son carved their own path of wealth. Jake's father, George Thomas, carved his way through construction and real estate.

Although George could have stuck a silver spoon in

his son's mouth, he intentionally went the other direction. George raised his only son, Jake, to be a hardworking man who takes care of business and his family, first and foremost. Jake grew up working dawn until dusk on the family farm, earning every single thing he received.

Jake would spend the little downtime that he had in the woods; hiking fishing and riding horses—a true country boy at heart. When he was old enough, his father taught him how to handle a gun and it wasn't long before Jake became a better shot than his father. He loved the sport of shooting. After a long day's work, Jake would pack a cooler and spend the evening shooting targets, improving his accuracy.

Jake joined the Army with one goal in mind—to become an elite Sniper. After graduating from Ranger School, he had to prove himself on the battlefield before even being considered for Sniper School.

After two lengthy deployments in Iraq and one in Afghanistan, Jake was accepted into Sniper school and graduated at the head of his class. He lived and breathed the military.

His social life was not uncommon for an elite Army Ranger. Lots of women, no strings attached. Exactly what he wanted. At six-foot-two, two hundred and thirty pounds, Jake had no problem getting women. He was blessed with the best of both his parents. His father's build, strength, and take no prisoner's attitude, and his mother's dark brown hair, bright blue eyes and unwavering perseverance. Jake had the rugged sexy thing going for him in every way possible.

He was never the class clown or the life of the party; he

was more of a wallflower that oozed a quiet, strong, killer confidence. The kind of confidence where you knew he could snap your neck in two seconds flat without so much as blinking an eye, and then steal your wife… and then your mom.

On his last tour in Iraq, he and his team were doing a routine perimeter check when their Humvee hit an IED on the side of the road.

Jake was thrown thirty-feet from the vehicle.

It wasn't until he woke up in the hospital the next day that he learned that not only was his partner killed, he had also shattered three discs in his back and would need invasive surgery, accompanied with an iron rod inserted down his spine.

After the surgery and months of therapy, although Jake felt one-hundred percent cured, the Army deemed him unfit for active service. They offered him many different desk positions, but nothing on the battlefield.

And then, another opportunity came his way. The FBI.

Special agent Mike Woodson sought Jake out for his impressive sharp-shooting skills, and offered him a position. A desk job for three years so he could learn the ropes before heading out in the field.

After spending a week considering the offer, Jake respectfully declined. Why? It wasn't in Jake's genes to sit behind a desk, not for a week, not for three years. He was built for action, for adventure, for active service.

After multiple conversations with Woodson, the FBI finally agreed to give Jake a trial run on a low risk surveillance mission in Arkansas, after completing a six-month crash course in undercover work. But, the message was clear—this was a *trial run* for Jake; if Jake failed to bring back actionable intel, he was out of a job. No second chances with the FBI. From his first day in Berry Springs, he would be given one week.

Jake accepted the challenge.

So far, the biggest challenge he'd had was keeping the mission a secret from his mother. This was urged by Woodson, practice he called it, for the real undercover work. Jake agreed because there was no need to make her worry, until the FBI officially offered him a position.

It had been less than forty eight hours since Jake had arrived in Berry Springs and he was already itching to get to work at his new job. Or, trial run job, at least.

Taking one last look at the rising sun, he kissed his mom on the top of the forehead and walked inside. After refilling his coffee, he opened his laptop and logged into his email. Quickly filtering out the nonsense, he paused on a classified email from Woodson, sent at three forty-nine in the morning.

Here we go.

3S Site, the subject read. The email was blank other than an attachment and *MW* written at the bottom. His pulse picked up as he opened the only attachment. Zooming in, he scanned the black and white quadrants of his first job.

"Jake, you want breakfast?"

He quickly minimized the email and pushed back his chair. "No, thanks." He flipped the laptop closed and walked into the kitchen. "There's a lot to be done around here today." He nodded out the window. "I'll start with the barn. Damn thing is about to fall apart."

As he strode out the front door, she called after him. "Alright, then. Don't forget to do some relaxing on your time off!"

༄

Katie woke up with a scream. Another bad dream.

She rolled over and glanced at the clock, six-thirty in the morning. Damn. Way too early.

Heart pounding and skin slicked with sweat, she took a few deep breaths. It was just a dream... just a dream.

She pushed herself off the mattress and padded to the kitchen. There was no way in hell she could go back to sleep, so she set the coffee to brew and stepped out on the back porch to inhale the fresh mountain air. Her gaze turned to the woods. Looking much less ominous in the early morning sun, she kicked herself for being such a wimp the night before, for the second time.

The fresh smell of coffee filled the air as she stretched her arms over her head. It was going to be a long day.

She walked back into the kitchen, poured herself a steaming cup and flipped open her laptop.

Fifty-one unread emails. Great. She scrolled down to the latest one from her partner, Bobby.

Hey boss, I hope everything's going smoothly. Remember, if you need anything at all, let me know. I've got some big news— we possibly have a job in North Carolina, I'm working out the details now. A construction crew thinks they found thousands' year old human remains on the Outer Banks. The gossip is already circling around The Lost Colony. Pretty exciting!

Will be ready to go as soon as you are.

BC

Katie's heart skipped a beat. She'd studied the Lost Colony in college and was always fascinated with the mystery. Over one hundred English settlers sailed to North Carolina in 1587, only to completely vanish from the face of the earth three years later.

She typed her response.

BC, Very exciting! Will get out of here as soon as I can, trust me! Give me three days.

She gulped her coffee and answered a few more emails, then shut it down. Dread filled her as she looked around the kitchen. It all felt so overwhelming, everything she had to do.

Her pulse picked up with anxiety, and she decided she needed to calm down, clear her head before tackling the long to-do list. Get focused.

She needed a jog. A jog always helped to clear her head. And then she'd get right to work.

She threw on her running gear and with the iPod screaming AC/DC, she began her workout with twenty pushups. Okay, ten. She'd work up to twenty. Pushups, sit-ups, lunges. Next, a good run to loosen up her muscles. The warm humidity coated her skin as she took off in a jog down the gravel driveway. It was going to be a hot one, for sure.

She was two miles into her run when she saw a woman crossing the dirt road up ahead. She slowed her pace and stopped.

"Maddie!"

Katie's neighbor, dressed in a pink terry cloth robe and slippers—despite the heat—turned and cocked her head.

"Well, I'll be... Katie Somers!" She reached out her delicate hand which was almost as shaky as her voice.

Catching her breath, Katie took Maddie's hand and gently squeezed it. "It's so good to see you."

Maddie had been Katie's neighbor since as long as she could remember. Becoming a widow at just forty years old, Maddie had continued to live alone in the old log cabin that her husband had built for her. With no children to lean on, Maddie took care of the house, the property and two horses, all on her own.

"Your mom called from England and told me you'd be here getting the house ready to sell." Maddie stepped in for a warm hug. "I'm so sorry, sweetheart. How are you holding up?"

"Thanks, I'm doing okay."

"How long are you here for?"

"A few days. I've been meaning to thank you for checking on the house from time to time, and for taking care of Greta."

"It's no problem at all. Harry loves the company." She looked past Katie. "That house needs a lot of work. I'm afraid it needs more tending to than I can offer, though."

"I'm going to work on it while I'm here."

"That's good, it's such a nice house." Her eyes suddenly lit up and a big smile crossed her face. "Hey, why don't you take Greta out while you're here?"

Katie hesitated. The last time she was on a horse was the worst day of her life.

Maddie pressed. "She really needs to get out of the fence, stretch her legs."

"I would, but, I have so much to do."

"Oh, come on, surly you could fit in a short break to see your horse?"

Guilt trip. Dammit. "Okay, you're right, it might be good to get out of the house for a bit."

Maddie clapped her hands together. "Great, I'll make apple-pie and you'll have some coffee when you come by."

Knowing how happy it made Maddie to have company, Katie didn't argue, although the apple-pie and pizza from last night was going to cost her a few more miles.

"Sounds good, Maddie."

"Okay, dear, see you soon!"

CHAPTER 7

KATIE GLANCED AT the antique clock on the wall as she walked into Maddie's kitchen. She'd lost track of time working on the house and it was much later in the afternoon than she intended.

"Sit, please. Make yourself at home, dear." Maddie grinned from ear to ear as she filled two cups with coffee. The ceramic mugs had the same kittens on them as did the curtains, hand towels and place settings. Funnily enough, Maddie didn't have any cats. "You'll have to excuse my excitement, I never get company anymore."

"I'm happy to be here, it's a much needed break for me."

Maddie handed Katie the steaming cup of coffee and placed cream and sugar in the center of the table.

"Thank you."

"You're very welcome. Now, tell me. How are things with you? With your mom being gone and all?"

Katie poured a dash of creamer and sipped her coffee. "I miss her... I wish she was here now, but, she seems happy in England." She looked down. "I understand her for running away. Even all the way across the globe."

Maddie reached across the table and laid a hand over Katie's. "Losing a child must be unbearable, but losing a sister is too." A moment of silence slid between them and Maddie swiftly changed the subject. "It's probably good she left this old town anyways... things are changing around these parts. Did you hear about the capitol building?"

"I saw it on the news. Have any new details come out?"

She shook her head, "Not that I've heard. A bomb threat! I mean, who would do that?"

"Probably some crazy kids."

"Exactly." Maddie sipped her coffee before going off on a rant. "Some crazy kids who probably grew up without any discipline what-so-ever. You know, times have changed, my dear. Things have changed. Hell, even the town has changed! I'll betcha the cops are a lot busier these days than when I was growing up. See, I didn't grow up in this entitled society like you kids do these days."

Katie smiled.

"Oh, no offense to you dear." She waved her hand in the air. "Oh, listen to me, going on and on. I told you, I never get company. I guess I have a lot bottled up."

"Well, you keep feeding me this fresh coffee, Maddie, and I'll listen to you for hours."

Maddie laughed, "You're so sweet, Katie. Always were." She glanced out the window. "Anyway, I heard the old Hamilton Estate sold to a widow recently. Just a few roads down. I'm hoping she might need someone to talk to just like I do."

"That mansion on the river?"

"Yep, sold to some rich lady from up north, so I hear."

"That place is enormous. I've seen it from the river."

"Way too much house for anyone if you ask me." As the oven dinged, Maddie gulped the rest of her coffee and slid out of her chair. "Fresh, homemade apple-pie, comin' up!"

An hour later, with her stomach filled to the brim with apple-pie, vanilla ice cream, and hot coffee, Katie saddled old Greta.

Maddie threw her a bottle of water before adjusting the ankle straps. "You're all set. And thanks, hon, Greta is so excited to stretch her legs."

"No problem at all, Maddie. I'll have her back before nightfall."

"Sounds good, dear."

With a click of her heels, Katie tapped the reigns and stepped out of the gate.

"Good Greta, good girl," she cooed as they walked through the field and jumped over the fence into the woods.

Nerves tickled her stomach as they stepped into the deep brush. This was the exact path she and Jenna had taken a year earlier.

She took a deep breath and for a moment wanted to turn around and go back. She pulled Greta to a stop and closed her eyes, listening to the sounds around her. She lifted her face to the sky and let the warmth of the sun wash over her.

Streaks of gold burst through the trees, as the last of the day's sun began to dip below the tallest mountain. Shadows danced on the ground. She estimated she had about an hour and a half of daylight left.

"Come on, girl, let's go." Exhaling, she gave Greta a light tap and they continued through the woods.

Everything was different. She grew up running on the trails, but now, a year after her sister's death, the familiar surroundings were just... different. Haunting, almost.

She tried to quiet her mind by focusing on the beauty around her when she came to a fork in the trail. Right, led up the mountain to the cliff. Left, down to the river. She hesitated, but couldn't ignore the pull she felt. Something was pulling her to the cliff... a nagging sixth sense was urging her to travel the steep trail up the mountain.

She took another moment to debate and finally clicked her heels and pulled Greta to the right, up the mountain. Her pulse picked up. Why the hell was she doing this?

A bumpy twenty minutes later, Greta stepped out of the woods and onto the large rock that marked the cliff.

She pulled the horse to a stop and her eyes locked on the very edge of the rock, where her sister tumbled to her death. Unable to fight it, tears filled her eyes as she looked around. This was the exact spot where she saw her sister for the last time. Where she left her, alone, on the rock.

She slid off the horse and walked as close to the edge as she could get, and her mind started racing.

It didn't make sense. Why would her sister crawl down to the very edge? And how, being on all fours, would she all of a sudden fall over?

Katie carefully stepped back and sat down on the rock, hugging her knees to her chest.

What seemed like an hour slid by while memories of her sister flowed through her mind, dancing from the last day she saw her, to memories of their childhood together.

She found herself smiling and almost laughing thinking of all the things they did when they were children, and all the trouble they got into while on their hikes. Then, she thought about life, her life, and what the hell she was doing with it.

She took a deep breath as the last of the bright, bold light of the setting sun streaked the sky. She smiled and said, "I love you, sister."

Time to head back.

She pushed herself off the rock when she heard something behind her. Greta let out a deep snort in response. She didn't remember passing anyone on the trail and would've heard someone coming up behind as she made her way up to the cliff.

Her body tensed from head to toe and an unexpected fear swept over her. She'd never felt scared in the woods. Her woods.

Looking down the steep ravine, she realized her options right now were limited. Very limited. It was either turn around and face whoever, or whatever it was, or jump.

All senses peaked; she slowly looked over her shoulder.

"Hi there." His voice was deep, and as smooth as a mug of hot chocolate on an icy winter night.

She turned.

Rays of glittering light outlined his large body, his face shadowed by a large tree. He sat atop a massive horse as black as coal with a German shepherd trailing behind him. She shaded her eyes from the setting sun and squinted to see more.

Her voice cracked, "Hello."

A light click of his heels sent his horse stepping closer

and out of the sun. Her stomach tickled as his face came into view. Shaggy dark brown hair framed a chiseled face with luscious lips and bright blue eyes. Eyes as blue as the sky. A gray T-shirt clung to his muscular chest and wide shoulders.

A knot formed in her throat as he slid off his horse.

"Beautiful view." He slowly stepped toward her, his unassuming eyes scanning her from head to toe.

"Yes, it is. Especially at sunset."

For a brief moment, they stared at each other. His eyes twinkled as he smiled, stepped forward and extended his hand. "I'm Jake."

She slid her fingers over his callused hand. "Katie."

"Katie," he replied as if approving her name. "You out here alone?"

Taking a moment to consider her answer, she glanced back at Greta and nodded. "Just me and my horse, Greta." The two horses took an interest in each other and began sniffing snouts. Katie eyed the magnificent black horse. "Beautiful horse." She stroked his mane. "Might be the biggest I've ever seen."

"I get that a lot." He grinned.

She smirked and rolled her eyes. So he was witty, okay.

He grabbed the horse's bridal, pulling him toward her. "He's a handful, but smart as a whip. His name's Butch. And, this is Shotsky."

"Hi there, Butch, Shotsky." She bent down and stroked the dogs head.

"He likes you. He's usually jumpy around strangers."

The tickle in her stomach turned to butterflies. She felt like a school girl as she smiled back.

He kept his eyes locked on her. "Are you from here?"

"Yes, born and raised, but only in town for a few days. I haven't been back in a decade."

"What brings you back?"

She looked down for a moment. "I'm getting my mom's house ready to sell." She hesitated and then looked up. He squinted, apparently sensing there was more to the story.

Time to change the subject. "You're not from around here, are you?"

"What makes you think I'm not from around here?"

She glanced down at his feet. "Your five hundred dollar hiking boots, without a scratch on them."

He looked down, grinned and looked back up. "And here I thought it was because I didn't say 'Howdy pardner' when I walked up."

She laughed.

"I'm from Montana."

"Montana? Long ways away. What brings you all the way to little Berry Springs?"

He searched her face, soaking in every line and curve. "Aside from the beauty?"

She felt her cheeks heat. Okay, so this guy was witty and smooth.

He continued, "My mom just moved here, so I'm here for a while, to help out."

Witty, smooth, *and* a loving son.

"Does she live on the mountain?"

He nodded. "Not too far from here."

"We're close then. I'm just off County Road 26." Why the hell did she tell him that?

Silence fell between them and he looked up at the sky. "Going to get dark soon."

She pulled Greta to her and adjusted the saddle. "I was just about to head back down the mountain."

"I'll join you."

She raised her eyebrows. Part of her wanted to jump at the opportunity to spend just one more minute with the handsome stranger, but the other part of her reminded herself that he was just that—a stranger.

"That's alright, I'll be fine."

"Steep descent in the dark."

She snorted, cocked her head. "Please. I could walk this trail with my eyes closed."

He crossed his arms over his chest. "I'd like to see that."

"I bet you would."

She was flirting.

He smiled. "Well, eyes open or closed, I was just about to head back down myself."

So... he would be traveling behind her whether she liked it or not. She raised her eyebrows and pretended to sound aloof, "Well, sounds like it's all planned out, then."

He gave a quick nod and stepped over to her as she turned to mount Greta. His large hands gripped her waist and hoisted her into the saddle as if she weighed ten pounds. Goosebumps broke out over her body. Bold move for a stranger but she liked it. "Thank you."

He smiled a playful smile and something sparked in his eye. Then, he mounted his horse and motioned to the trail, "Ladies first."

Shadows from the fading sun danced across the trail as they stepped off the rock and into the darkening woods.

They walked in silence, listening to the breeze blow through the trees and the noisy critters making their last rounds before nightfall.

About halfway down the mountain, Jake halted behind her.

Katie turned to see Shotsky staring into the dark woods, his hair standing on its end. A low growl vibrated from his throat.

"What's going on?"

"I don't know." He peered into the dark woods, his face pulled tight with intensity. After a moment he guided Butch off the trail, following Shotsky.

Katie looked around, warily. "What are you doing? It's getting too dark."

"Stay there, we'll be right back," he yelled as he faded into the darkness.

Katie looked over her shoulder. Yeah, right, she wasn't just going to sit there waiting while it gets dark.

She blew out an exhale. "Damn boys. Tsk-tsk, come on Greta, let's go." She clicked her heels and pulled Greta into the woods, falling into step behind Butch and Jake.

The deeper in the woods they rode, Shotsky got more and more anxious. A sudden feeling of dread washed over Katie. Her sixth sense—the one her mother told her never to ignore—was yelling, no; make that *screaming* at her. She scanned the woods around them and then looked forward to see Jake looking over his shoulder, his steely eyes staring at her. His voice low and serious, he said, "Stay close."

Eyebrows pushed together, she nodded.

Suddenly, Shotsky jumped in front of a large bush, his

71

growl intensifying. Jake pulled Butch to a stop and peered over the bush.

A million flies buzzed overhead. Buzzards flapped their wings angrily in the surrounding trees. The air was thick and heavy... heavy with something. Something bad.

The expression on Jakes face made the hair on the back of Katie's neck stand up. For a moment, she considered turning around and running. From what, she wasn't sure.

Jake dismounted the horse, glanced back at her, "Stay there." His eyes were sharp and intense, nothing like when they met just moments ago.

She watched him crouch down and pull a gun out of his ankle holster. A gun. Why the hell was he carrying a gun?

Slowly, silently he stepped over the bush. His face fierce, he looked down at something that Katie couldn't see from her vantage point. She watched him bend down, slowly stand back up, draw his gun and do a three-hundred sixty degree turn, scanning the woods.

Her pulse spiked. "Jake, what is it?"

His eyes met hers as he lowered his gun. "A body."

"A *body*? What? I don't think I heard you."

Looking past her he repeated himself, "A body."

Her eyes widened. "A *dead* body?"

"Yes. Stay there."

Yeah, right. Katie dismounted and tiptoed to the edge of the bush.

"I told you to stay there."

His words faded in her ears as she peered over. The smell singed her nose. The sight of it blurred her vision.

Her stomach plummeted as she bent over and began heaving apple-pie, ice cream and coffee.

"Whoa, hey, it's okay, it's okay." Like a flash of lightning, he was by her side.

Dizzy, vision clouded, she wiped her mouth and grabbed his arm. "I'm sorry, I'm sorry."

"It's okay. Just breathe. It's okay."

She concentrated on his soothing voice as he put an arm around her.

"Can you stand?"

"Yes, yes, I'm embarrassed, I'm…" still gripping him, she lost her words as she looked back down at the body.

Not two feet from her lay a naked woman, maybe in her mid-twenties, gutted at the waist with her internal organs spilling from her body, where nature's creatures had obliged themselves for breakfast. Half of her gray, paper-thin skin was ripped away, exposing bone with gnaw marks. Strands of matted hair sprawled across her head and neck and portions of her face had been torn away, exposing her skeleton. One eye had been pecked out; the other stared lifelessly at the sky.

Katie blinked away the tears in her eyes. She wanted to look away from the gruesome sight, but couldn't.

The woman's arms and legs were splayed out as if she were an innocent child about to make a snow angel. Maggots slithered inside and outside of the body.

Feeling another wave of nausea, Katie slammed her eyes shut. "Oh my God, oh my God."

"Okay, come over here."

She gripped Jake's arm as he led her a few steps away.

"She's dead. Oh my God, she's dead."

"Yes."

She looked up and met his eyes. "How long do you think she's been out here?"

"I don't think very long."

"What... who would do this?" Katie looked past him and into the woods. "Oh my God, do you think whoever did it is still out here?"

"I don't know." He pulled out a cell phone from his pocket, but paused before releasing her arm. "Are you okay to stand?"

She slowly nodded.

"Okay, I need to make a few phone calls." He let go of her, leaving her feeling extremely vulnerable.

"There's no reception out here. I can... I can go back down the trail and try to find someone."

"No." His voice sharp. "You stay right here with me."

She nodded and looked up at the sky. "The light's fading. The light is fading, Jake. It's going to be pitch black in about thirty minutes."

He nodded and stepped away as his phone call connected.

CHAPTER 8

A NOT-SO-QUICK TWENTY MINUTES later, the roar of police sirens echoed through the woods.

Katie blew out an exhale, "Thank God, they're here. I'll go to the trail and meet them." She turned on her heel when Jake stopped her.

"No. We'll go together." By his tight expression, she could tell that was not negotiable. He firmly grabbed her hand, led her to her horse and guided her onto the saddle. Holding Greta's bridal, he led them through the woods, with Shotsky close on his heels.

As he maneuvered the horse through the brush, Katie watched his confident, strong movements. Light beads of perspiration had his T-shirt melting onto his tanned skin. She could see every muscle in his back flex with each movement he made. He looked like a man on a mission. A man who was completely in control.

Although she had only known him for what seemed like minutes, she had already seen two very different sides of him. A charismatic, friendly Jake. And now, a man with sheer resolve, acute awareness and a deadly calmness. Right now, he seemed to be the type of man that could take on the whole world with his bare hands.

She cocked her head and glanced down at his ankle. Why does he carry a gun? Should she be scared of him? *Is she scared of him?*

They stepped onto the trail.

"Hey!" Attempting to hide his labored breath from jogging up the trail, Police Chief David McCord picked up his pace as soon as he saw them. His eyes locked on Jake's as he sized him up.

Small town cop turned police chief, David McCord didn't take kindly to strangers. Born and raised in Berry Springs, he'd spent twenty years on the force before being promoted to chief. That was ten years ago. And, according to the town gossip, he'd been at that desk for nine years too long. He was a pudgy, six-foot-tall, balding man, with a sharp nose and three divorces under his belt.

Katie remembered him instantly. McCord was in the station the day of Jenna's death. Although he didn't personally speak with Katie that day, she remembered him barking out orders.

Squaring his shoulders and puffing out his chest, the chief stepped up to Jake.

"Police Chief McCord." As he extended his hand, Shotsky let out a low growl.

"It's okay, Shots." He shook the chief's hand. "Jake Thomas.

"Hey, boys!" Running up the hill at an impressive pace, Officer Dean Walker stepped next to McCord. Wearing a navy police T-shirt and tactical pants, Walker was a handsome, muscular, southern boy with dark hair and penetrating green eyes. Dean was fresh out of the academy and on his second year on the force. McCord made the introduction.

"Officer Walker, this is Jake Thomas, who phoned in the body, and…" he finally glanced over at Katie, "Katie *Somers*? I haven't seen you since last year." His eyes lingered a moment too long. "I don't think I ever got to personally tell you how sorry I was about your sister."

"Thanks, Chief McCord."

Impatient—and not a fan of small talk—Jake stepped forward. "Officer Walker, nice to meet you. The body's about thirty feet in." He nodded toward the woods.

"Let's take a look."

Jake and McCord started into the woods, side by side. Officer Walker followed closely behind, and Katie on Greta behind them.

Jake walked over the rugged terrain as if he'd been through it a hundred times. "We're going to lose light soon."

McCord glanced up at the sky, "Yep, I'd say you're right. Let me see what we've got first, then I'll call up a team."

Jake stepped up to the bush that hid the body and paused. "I walked right here," he motioned to the side, "but, you'll want to step around this way, so you don't contaminate the scene."

McCord eyed Jake for a moment, giving him a look that might intimidate most men, before stepping around the bush. The only thing more obvious than Jake's disdain for small talk was McCord's untrusting demeanor toward the stranger who called in a body.

Still mounted on Greta and staying a few feet behind,

Katie watched McCord's face as he looked down. He took a moment before speaking and then muttered to himself, "Son-of-a-bitch." He turned to Officer Walker. "Get the team up here immediately. And start roping this off. No one steps in this space until everyone gets here."

"Yes, sir." Walker stepped away from the group to make the call.

Shaking his head, McCord took a few steps back and whispered under his breath, "*Dammit.*"

"You know her?"

The chief's head snapped up, his eyes narrowed as he looked at Jake. "It's Jake *Thomas*, correct?"

A swift nod in response.

"I don't recognize the name. You're not from around here."

"Montana."

McCord pulled out a cigarette and lit the tip. After a long inhale, he asked, "And what would bring a boy from Montana to little Berry Springs?"

Not breaking eye contact, or his no-bullshit tone, Jake replied, "My mother."

"She lives here?"

"Just moved here."

McCord glanced at Katie, and back to Jake. "And you just came out for a hike?"

"Yes."

"This your first time here?"

"Yes."

"How do you know Katie?"

Katie's heart started to beat a little faster.

Without answering, Jake looked at Katie. She got the message. McCord was obviously skeptical, at best, of Jake and didn't believe a word that came out of his mouth. He'd be more inclined to believe a local. So, she spoke up. "I just met him, literally, about thirty minutes ago."

"So, you two really don't know each other at all, huh?"

"That's right, I guess."

"You just ran into each other?"

"Yes."

"And what you were doing on the trails this evening, Miss Somers?"

"Same as Jake, just hiking with Greta here." She nervously began to stroke Greta's mane.

McCord took a pull off of his cigarette. "What brings you back in town?"

"My mom's selling her house. I'm getting it cleaned up, and everything ready."

"The house you grew up in?"

"Yes."

"Wow, that place needs a lot of TLC to get ready to sell. You must be pretty busy."

She nodded.

"But not too busy for a leisurely hike."

Jake's gaze toward McCord turned ice-cold. He shifted his weight, moving closer to Katie. A protective stance.

Officer Walker ran up, breaking the silence. "Everyone's on their way." Sensing the tension, he looked from McCord, to Jake, to Katie, to Greta—who grunted as if on cue—then back at McCord again. "Everything alright here?"

McCord nodded and looked back at Jake. "We're going to need you to step aside now. And we'll also need the both of you to make a formal statement about what you saw today."

Jake looked down at the rotting body. "This is what we saw. That's it."

"It's protocol, Mr. Thomas."

The two men engaged in a final stare-off before Jake turned away.

Darkness had begun to fall on woods. Twilight cast an eerie blue glow through the trees. The impending blackness felt like an evil power about to take over. A thick, dark cloud of evil, sweeping through the woods, that couldn't be stopped.

It would be completely dark in less than ten minutes. Katie glanced up at the stars beginning to twinkle in the sky. What a hell of an evening.

A dead body. A dead woman in Berry Springs.

Her stomach rolled with the thought that bad luck seemed to be following her. What the hell had she gotten herself into?

She looked toward the trail, plotting her escape. Getting down the mountain in the dark was going to be tricky, not to mention creepy.

"Do you need to call anyone?"

"No, I just need to get Greta back soon."

Jake nodded and glanced back at McCord who was whispering with Walker. Jake shook his head, and under his breath, said, "Here we go," as Walker walked up to them.

Walker addressed Katie first. "You doing okay, Miss?…"

"Somers."

"That's right. Sorry."

"It's okay, and yeah, I'm okay. A little shaken up."

"Must've been a hell of a surprise walking up on this." He looked around, "Speaking of, what were ya'll doing off the trail?"

Jake stepped between the officer and Katie. "My dog," he nodded over to Shotsky, "guided us over here."

"Your dog did?"

"Yes."

"Must be a smart dog."

"Yes."

"He just guided you right over to a dead body?"

"Yes."

"Alright." A muscle in Walkers jaw twitched as he scribbled on a pad of paper. "And this was when?"

"About forty minutes ago."

"Alright," He looked at Katie, "And how did you and Mr. Thomas meet?"

"On the cliff, over there. He walked up as I was about to leave."

"And what did you say you were doing in town?"

"We've already been over this with the Chief," Jake said.

Meeting his sharp tone, Walker narrowed his eyes. "Am I keeping you from something more important, Mr. Thomas?"

"You're wasting your time with these questions, Officer Walker. So, to speed thing up, I'll help you out. As I told McCord, I'm in town helping my mother move into her new house. To acclimate myself with the area, I took her horse out for a ride, where I met Katie for the first time, and then a dead body. Next, you'll ask me what I do for a living. I'm an Army Ranger, currently on leave."

Walker raised an eyebrow but before he could respond,

his attention was drawn to the commotion on the trail. Evidently, the "team" was here.

He took one more glance toward Jake, then turned and whistled.

From the trail, the flashlights pointed toward the sound as the team made their way through the woods.

"Walker, hey. What we got?" A short, stocky woman with fiery red hair and green eyes stomped up to the scene.

"Young woman, deceased… gutted."

Her green eyes widened. "Gutted?"

"Gutted."

"Let's have a look-see."

Katie watched as Walker led the woman to the brush.

McCord turned and nodded in salutation, "Jessica."

"McCord."

All eyes were glued on the town's Medical Examiner as she stepped over the police tape and peered over the twisted bushes.

Her head snapped up. "Dammit, who vomited here?"

Katie shrunk in the saddle as the woman glanced back at her.

Disgusted—more so with the vomit than with the rotting corpse—she shook her head and said under her breath, "Contaminated my damn crime scene."

Born and raised in Berry Springs, Jessica Heathrow had a ball-busting attitude and a vulgar vocabulary to match, but was tolerated by everyone for her competence and accurate instincts at a crime scene. A self-proclaimed workaholic, Jessica held the position of the Medical Examiner for fifteen years, and although she technically had an assistant, it was widely known that she did ninety-nine percent of the work that was sent to the office.

Her stone-cold expression didn't change as she sat down her bag, slipped a pair of blue booties over her shoes and pulled on latex gloves. With not so much as a flinch, she knelt down by the dead body. As her eyes analyzed she said, "Where the hell are my lights?"

"Here!" An officer jogged through the bush and close behind him, a rugged looking man in a blue button up and khakis.

"Damn, that's a hike. Jessica! What the hell are you doing? Back up! Pictures first."

The redhead glanced up with fire spilling from her eyes. "Jameson, maybe if you'd get your fat ass here sooner, the whole fucking team wouldn't have to wait on you."

Detective Eric Jameson, an Army veteran and Berry Springs police officer turned Detective, didn't even break his stride. "Oh, I'm sorry Jess, I know you Medical Examiners are usually kicking back at happy hour by now."

She rolled her eyes as she pushed up to a stance, "Go fuck yourself, Jameson. I do more work in an hour than you do in a day."

Jameson seemed to habitually ignore her as he walked up to the police tape. He peered past the bush and the blood drained from his face. Recognition flickered in his eyes and he looked up at the Chief. "Oh, shit."

McCord pursed his lips together, expression grim, and nodded.

Jameson took a second to compose himself, then quickly set up the lights and began taking pictures from all angles. The grotesque scene illuminated as if it were a stage in a theater, a horror play in its final act.

Not one to miss much, Jessica pulled McCord aside.

"You not telling me something, McCord?"

"What do you mean?" McCord lit his third cigarette.

Jessica waved the smoke away. "What was that glance? Between you and Jameson?"

He took a long drag, and looked down at the body. "You don't recognize her?"

"Half her face has been eaten off, McCord."

"Look at the other half, her size, color of her hair."

It took a few seconds, but then as if someone slapped her in the face, her mouth dropped open and eyes rounded. "Oh my God... do you think?"

He shrugged. "You'll be the one to determine that, but, hell of a coincidence."

Eyes bugging, she looked down at the body. "I can't believe I didn't put it together. She looks to be over twenty-four hours deceased." She shook her head. "That's about how long Amy Duncan's been missing, isn't it?"

"Yep."

"Oh my God, where's Carl?"

"I advised him to take some time off after she went missing. Damn near everyone in town knew about the affair. Told him to lay low for a bit."

Jessica glanced back at Jake and Katie, who were being questioned, again, by Walker. "I'm guessin' they found her?"

"Yep."

"Don't recognize them."

"Boy's not from around here. Girl's Katie Somers."

"Katie Somers? Ain't seen her in a decade."

"Well, everyone's about to know she's back, I'm guessin'."

"They make a statement?"

"Walkers working on that."

She nodded and looked back down at the body. "Well, shit, man. I'll make this top priority."

"Yes, you will."

"Hey, Jameson, come get this." Officer Walker motioned the Detective over to a small patch of dirt a few feet from the body.

"What you got?" Jameson carefully made his way over and knelt down.

"Shoeprint." He pointed to the soil. "See there?"

Jameson squinted and leaned forward. "Yeah, yeah, I do. Move back and shine the light." He began snapping pictures. "Not bad. Can even make out the tread."

"Looks like a boot, a lot of wear." Jessica peered over them, patiently waiting for Jameson to finish photographing so she could get her hands on the body.

"Agreed. It's a good mark." He lowered the camera and bit his lip, in deep thought.

"We had that rain two days ago, then the heat wave."

"Ah, that's right… whoever this is must've stepped here after the rain, but before things dried up."

"Hate to burst your bubble Jameson, but, hunters, hikers; anyone could have made that track."

He paused a beat. "How old you think the body is?"

"Just told McCord, I think around twenty-four hours, but of course, that's just from the three seconds I got to look at her before you pulled me off." She squatted down, and lowering her voice, asked, "Do you think it's Amy?"

Jameson reached in his pocket, pulled out a small yellow flag and placed it next to the print then turned to Jessica. "God, I hope not... For Carl's sake. We need to get a cast of this print."

"Finish pictures first so I can get to work, then cast."

"You got it."

After a few minutes, Jameson finished taking pictures and Jessica got to work.

Katie watched in awe as the scene unfolded around her. She strained to listen to the cop talk, but between the night critters and cicadas, she couldn't hear more than muffled whispers. Jake stood stoically, expressionless, soaking in every detail of the horrific scene, but she noticed that every minute or so he scanned the dark woods surrounding them. Did he think whoever did this was watching?

Hunched over the body, Jessica yelled out over her shoulder, "Someone come here and adjust the light."

McCord turned, "What do you see?"

Walker stepped over and pulled the light closer to the body as Jessica carefully lifted the left arm. "She's been branded."

"Branded?"

"Yeah." She nodded. "Yes, I think so."

"Could it be a tattoo?"

"Not unless the new cool thing is to do *burn* designs into the skin." She paused. "Which hell, wouldn't surprise me." She pulled a magnifying glass from her bag and leaned closer. "Can you see?"

Covering his nose with a handkerchief, McCord leaned

forward and peered at the small symbol burned into the woman's rotting flesh.

∽

An hour later, Jake had insisted on walking—or riding alongside—Katie home to make sure she was safe. If nothing else, his mom taught him to be a gentleman. Not much made her prouder than to see her son open a door for a woman, or help an elderly lady carry groceries to her car. Jake did it habitually, without blinking an eye; or giving the woman in need a second thought.

But, something about this was different, and he wasn't sure why. There was more to his offer to walk Katie home than simply being an obligatory gentleman. True, he found her extremely attractive, but it surprised him that something intrigued him about her as well.

The moonlight cut through the trees, dancing like stars across her body as she rode horseback in front of him. With each step of the horse, her body swayed side to side and his eyes greedily soaked in every angle of her curves. He searched his thoughts for something to say to her... any kind of small talk, but came up short. This also surprised him. He never had trouble talking to a woman. Why was she different?

So, instead of small talk, he focused on the view ahead of him and the sound of the gravel crunching underneath the horse's hooves.

Despite the grotesque scene that lay before them an hour earlier, Jake found his mind wandering, lustfully. How could he not, with that sultry body swaying side to side ahead of him? He was a man, after all and she really was beautiful. Not Homecoming queen or cheerleader beautiful, but a kind of unassuming, natural beauty that is rare to find. The kind of beauty he favored, and fell hard for.

Jake had only had his heart broken once. One time. And, that was enough for him. He'd allowed himself to fall hard and fast for the Captain of the cheerleading squad, only to find out that she was more interested in the family money than she was in him. Since that earth-shattering break-up, he'd built a wall around his heart and kept his head on a swivel when it came to women. Aside from that, he traveled too much to put enough effort in a relationship to make it stick. And now, his travels would only become more extensive if this whole FBI thing panned out.

A cool breeze cut through the humidity, sweeping Katie's hair across her face as she glanced over her shoulder.

Their eyes locked.

Yes, I'm still here, right behind you. You're safe.

He watched her look forward, wait a beat and then turn back around.

"My neighbor's house is just up ahead," she gestured to a small hill, "I'm fine, you can head back."

"How do you plan on getting to your house after dropping the horse off?"

A minute ticked by.

"I had planned on walking back… I didn't think I'd be out past dark."

"How long a walk?"

"Two miles, at the most."

"That's a long walk, alone, in the dark."

No response.

"Well," he reached down and patted Butch's neck, "Butch won't mind the extra weight." *Dammit*, he cringed, that didn't come out right. Another thing his mother taught him was to never address a woman's weight. Maybe she didn't hear? Her eyes rolled as she turned forward. Yep, she heard.

They rode in silence up the hill and after securing Greta in the stable, Katie walked up to him with defiance marked all over her face.

"I'm fine you know, I used to jog this road all the time."

He cocked his head, "Funny, I'm sure those were her last words." He nodded toward the woods where they found the body.

There was no missing the eye roll this time. With a huff, she stepped up to Butch. And as she did so, Jake smirked, slid off and then hoisted her up and then mounted in front of her.

Excitement tingled in him as their bodies touched. Her thighs fit perfectly around his backside like a piece of a puzzle.

"Hold on."

As she wrapped her arms around him, her soft breasts pressed into his back. He reached back, grabbed her hand and pulled it closer. "Hold on tighter."

She looped her fingers and squeezed around him.

He clicked his heels and together, they galloped down the hill onto the dark dirt road.

What seemed like minutes later, she leaned forward and said, "Up to the right."

Jake pulled Butch up the steep hill to the decrepit

house. No woman he'd ever met would stay a single night in that house, alone.

They stopped at the porch steps and her arms lingered around him for just a moment, before she released and slid off. He looked down at her, and she up at him. Did she want him to come in? Perhaps he should offer?

Before he could solidify a clear thought, she said, "Thank you for getting me home."

"No problem."

Pause.

"Good night."

He watched her walk up the steps, unlock the door and close it behind her, and something more than lust stirred in him as he turned and rode away.

CHAPTER 9

KATIE SHUT THE door, put the full weight of her back against it and closed her eyes. She knew she wouldn't be able to get the image of the gutted women out of her head for a long time. Who was she? Who would do that to her? Who *murdered* her? She was young. A young woman with her whole life ahead of her. An ice-cold chill ran up her spine at that thought. Katie was a young woman herself. A woman who had seen two corpses over the last year. Her sister's, and now, another woman. This kind of stuff isn't supposed to happen in sleepy Berry Springs.

Murder doesn't happen here. Right?

She opened her eyes, flicked the lights and walked into the kitchen. She'd left all the windows in the house open, but thanks to the humid summer night, not even the slightest breeze made its way inside. It felt suffocating. Her head hurt. Her neck hurt. Her whole body ached from sitting horseback for hours. What a hell of a night.

She glanced at the clock. Ten o'clock in the evening. Yep, definitely time for a drink. She retrieved a wine glass from the cupboard and poured herself a hefty glass of red wine.

Leaning against the counter, her thoughts drifted from the murdered woman in the woods, to Jake. The *man* she found in the woods.

She took a deep sip.

She pictured the gun in his ankle holster. Who the hell was this guy? Why was he carrying a gun? Sure, this was Arkansas and almost everyone carried a gun, but it still surprised her. He wasn't out hunting, after all. He said he was just *acclimating himself with the area*?

An Army Ranger. It didn't surprise her. He looked like a military man. A strong, confident solider, with the most beautiful blue eyes she'd ever seen.

She looked out the kitchen window into the darkness and felt a slight surge of energy as the buzz from the wine kicked in. Restless, she began pacing the house, walking from one room to the next. She made her way into the den and her gaze drifted to her sister's laptop sitting in the corner of the room. Exactly where she had left it a year ago.

After a quick moment of hesitation, she picked up the computer and sank into the couch.

In the days after her sister's death, Katie hadn't even thought about going through her computer, closing her deceased sister's accounts and social media sites. She probably should have, but those few days had been a blur.

She opened the screen and pushed the power button.

The computer buzzed to life, breaking the silence in the house. Her finger trailed the small pad and clicked on the Internet browser.

Her sister's email account popped onto the screen.

Never one to snoop, she started to close it down, but, instead, she decided to look. She slowly moved the mouse to the inbox and, taking a deep breath, clicked.

Three hundred two unread emails. Holy smokes. Most were spam, some were creditors informing her of unpaid bills, some were from her distant friends.

And then, she saw it.

Her stomach dropped to her feet. The email was dated one day before Jenna's death.

Eyes wide, she lingered on the subject before clicking the message open.

Jenna,

Meet me tonight, ten o'clock, Pipers Pub. We'll nail down the plan for tomorrow. Looking forward to it.

David

David?

The email was from David McCord, the chief of police.

Katie's mouth fell open as she stared at the message. Jenna and David? *Jenna and David?*

She re-read the message three times. Why were they meeting? What plans for the next day? That would be the day that she died!

Her mind raced. Was it a date? Had they possibly been having an affair? Did Jenna's husband know? Is that really why they divorced?

She looked back at the date the email was received— yes, just one day before Jenna's death.

After reading the email one more time, she scrolled through the rest of her sister's messages looking for something else from McCord, but only found more spam, more of the same. Nothing else from him.

She clicked into the deleted email folder. Empty.

Taking a deep breath, she reopened the email and read it again. Her heart raced in her chest as she remembered seeing McCord in the station on the day of Jenna's death. She closed her eyes and searched her memory trying to remember if he looked sad, angry... or guilty. That day was still a blur, but one thing that did stick in her brain was that he stayed as far away from Katie as he could. He never even acknowledged her.

After a few more sips of wine, the shock of the email was replaced with anger. Was McCord somehow involved? Does he know something? After all, he was the one who signed off on the final assessment that Jenna *accidentally* tumbled to her death, falling off the cliff she'd been on a million times.

She felt heat rising to the top of her head as she clenched her jaw and considered calling him.

No. No, she needed to assess, to let the situation soak in. She snapped the laptop closed and pushed off the couch.

Anxious now, she ran her fingers through her hair and began pacing, again.

What a night. What a fucking night.

A plethora of emotions zipped through her body. She felt like she was going to explode.

She found herself pacing aimlessly down the hall and walking into Jenna's bedroom. Her eyes filled with tears, but none fell. She walked over to her overnight bag, unzipped the inner pocket and pulled out a small zip lock bag. Carefully, she opened it—as she had done a million times over the last year—and pulled out the white, pearl button. The button she found on the rock the day her sister died. Rolling it around in her fingers, she closed her eyes as the images from that day flashed through her head.

Her stomach rolled and she suddenly felt nauseous, dizzy. Turning on her heel, she ran to the kitchen, poured herself a glass of ice-cold water and gulped it down. She pressed the cold glass to her forehead and closed her eyes.

What the hell was happening?

She was used to being able to control every aspect of her life, but not now. She slid down the wall and sat on the cold kitchen floor.

What seemed like an hour passed when the silence of the house was broken by a noise outside. She lifted her head off the wall, sat the half empty bottle of wine on the floor and listened. Her stomach dropped when she heard it again, this time closer to the house.

She looked up at the dim light on in the kitchen, then out the window. From outside, there was no doubt whoever, or whatever, could see right into the house. She might as well have a spotlight on her and a sign that says: *I'm all alone, come get me.* Crouching to her hands and knees, she crawled across the kitchen, reached up the wall and flicked the light off. The room went dark.

Are the doors locked? Did she remember to lock the doors? Yes, she locked the doors. Right?

More noise outside. Where the hell was it coming from? An animal maybe?

Dammit Katie, it's probably just a deer, toughen up.

But… what if it wasn't?

A knife. She should get a knife. She crab walked across the kitchen to the boxes marked *UTENSILS*. As quietly as she could, she opened the flaps of the box, carefully felt around inside and pulled out a carving knife.

A light breeze blew through the house.

Creak…

The porch swing slowly swung back and forth.

Her pulse pounded.

With all of her senses peaked, she strained to listen for more noise.

Silence.

She grabbed her phone off the counter, and with knife in hand, she tiptoed to the den, which would allow her to hear anything throughout the house. She balled up on the floor, back against the wall and listened.

A cricket sang in perfect repetition outside the front window. She closed her eyes, took a deep breath and focused on the sound, trying to steady her breathing.

It was going to be a long night.

⤜

"What do you think?" Jameson asked, as he and McCord scaled the steps to the police station.

"My gut tells me it's her."

Jameson shook his head. "Are you going to call him now?"

The men pushed through the front doors and made their way through the bull pen, to the back offices.

"Yeah. Yeah, I think so."

"It's late."

McCord broke his stride and turned toward Jameson. He snapped, "Wouldn't you want to know? No matter what damn time it was?"

Jameson held up his hands as if to surrender. "Hey, I'm just saying that maybe we should wait until Jessica makes an official ID. The man's been through enough, he's at his breaking point. Shit, McCord, the chick that everyone knows he was having an affair with, suddenly goes missing. Now she's dead. I don't even want to imagine the hell his wife is giving him."

"Yeah, well, life's a bitch, Jameson." His voice reeked of irritation.

"It sure is." Jameson shrugged and glanced down at his watch. "I'll have Walker write up the report from tonight and send the cast off to the lab first thing in the morning."

McCord nodded and before stepping into his office, he paused and said, "The cast should give us the shoe size and approximate height and weight of the suspect, correct?"

"Assuming that the print belongs to the suspect, yes."

He narrowed his eyes. "Have Walker get those measurements from our boy Jake Thomas as well."

"Yes, sir."

"Also, he said he's an Army Ranger on leave. Confirm that."

"You got it."

McCord turned and stepped into his office. The red light on his answering machine flashed angrily at him, as it always did. Someone always needed something.

He blew out a breath and glanced at the clock. Eleven o'clock. They'd been at the site for over three hours, finding nothing more than a shoeprint, which was something, at least.

He looked down at his phone. Should he call? Yes, of course he should. Taking a deep breath, he sunk into his chair, picked up the phone and dialed the number.

"Hello?" He winced. The wife answered, and she definitely was not asleep.

"Hi Suzie, it's Chief McCord."

A moment passed, then, as cold as ice she said, "Hello, Chief."

"Is Carl available?"

"Hold on."

McCord listened to the muffled voices, and then finally the phone was handed over.

"Hey, McCord."

"Hey, Carl. Sorry to call so late."

"It's alright." No, it wasn't. "What's going on?"

"I thought you'd want to know... we found a body up on Summit Mountain."

Silence.

"A young woman, brown hair, small build," he cleared his throat, "looks like her."

Silence.

"Jessica's already bagged her up and is making her top priority."

A solid minute of dead air ticked by, then, with a cracking voice, Carl asked, "You think it's her?"

Pause. "Not sure yet."

"How'd she die?"

McCord took a moment to choose his words carefully before responding. He decided that it was probably best to leave out the fact she was gutted and branded. "It looks like foul play."

"Oh my God," Carl whispered. Another few seconds ticked by. "McCord," there was a panic to his voice now, "Oh my God, I know what this looks like. I didn't do it. You know that, right? I didn't do it." He lowered his voice, "You have to know that."

"I know, buddy." But, did he really know? Was he really sure? "Just tell me one thing." He looked down at his desk, embarrassed for what he had to ask, "Had you been with her lately?"

"… Yes."

The knot in McCord's stomach tightened. Carl's DNA would no doubt show up on the autopsy report.

"Okay," he took a deep breath, "We'll have the I.D. over the next few days, and I'll call you immediately."

"Okay."

"Until then, it's probably best to just stay at home."

"Yes, sir."

"Tell Suzie I'm sorry for calling so late. Bye, Carl."

He hung up and sank back in his chair, staring at the phone. He took another deep breath, leaned forward, picked up the phone, and made the call that was always the hardest.

"Hello?"

"Hi, Mrs. Duncan, it's Chief McCord."

"Oh my God, did you find her?"

"No, not yet. But… I wanted to tell you that we did find a young woman, deceased on Summit Mountain tonight. We'll make an official I.D. as soon as possible, but I wanted to let you know first, before you hear it on the news or anything."

A gasp, followed by the clanging of the phone tumbling to the ground. A minute passed.

"I'm... I'm sorry, I dropped the phone. Do... Do you think it's her?"

"I don't know ma'am, but you'll be the first to know."

"Thank you, Chief McCord. Please call us immediately."

"Yes, ma'am."

CHAPTER 10

HEAD THROBBING, KATIE poured coffee into Jenna's *I heart NY* mug. She had been unceremoniously awakened at dawn by her cell phone screaming at her, only to pick it up to be told by her partner Bobby, that he had officially booked the North Carolina dig and was just waiting on her to return to get started. Which was great news, but added pressure that she sure as hell didn't need right now.

She sipped her coffee and reflected on the horrific events of the day before. She still couldn't get the image of the dead woman out of her head, or the very sexy man she'd met. And, to top it all off, she uncovered a mysterious email sent to her sister from the chief of police, right before her death.

What a hell of a trip it was turning out to be.

Coffee in hand, she made her way to the porch and sat on the swing. The fresh scent of dawn perfumed the air. As she sipped and stared blankly into the woods, she made her first plan for the day. Forget about yesterday and get everything packed up and delivered to the thrift store. She needed to get the hell out of Berry Springs as quickly as possible. Two more days, tops.

She gulped the last bit of caffeine in her cup, promptly refilled it and made her way into the living room to attack the snarl of wires surrounding the TV.

The hours passed quickly and she had just taped the last box in the den when her cell phone rang.

"Hello?"

"Hey girl, it's Brit."

"Oh, hey. How are you?"

"Doing good. It was so good running into you at Gino's the other night... I just wanted to check up on you, how you doing?"

She looked around the cluttered room, "Okay, just working on getting everything ready to take to the thrift store today."

"It must be hard for you being out there all alone, I'm so sorry you've had to deal with it all."

"Thanks." She hesitated. Brit didn't know the half of what she was dealing with, but considering Brit was a known gossip, she decided to keep the dead body, sexy stranger and mystery email out of the conversation.

"You don't want to talk about it. I understand. But, you've got to eat right? Take a break and let's do lunch."

Katie blew out a breath. "I really can't, I've got so much to do."

"I know you do, but you need a break. An emotional break. No heavy talk, I promise. And I'll fill you in on all the town gossip while we're at it. Doesn't that sound fun?"

Lunch. Well, she *was* hungry. And maybe some gossip and a laugh or two might be exactly what she needed. "Alright, you're on."

"Great! Twelve-thirty, Donny's Diner, sound good to you?"

"Sure, see you then."

"Okay!"

Katie clicked off her phone and was surprised at the nerves that tickled her stomach. She didn't want to run into anyone, or talk about her sister, or the conspiracy theories.

She glanced out the window. The bushes that lined the house were already wilting under the hot summer sun and the humidity had doubled since she woke. Feeling empathetic for the bushes, she wiped the sweat from her forehead.

She needed a shower and a break from thinking about death.

Two hours later, Katie slid into a parking spot on the town square, a few doors down from the diner. Flipping down the sun shade, she checked her lipstick, for the third time. Dammit, why was she so nervous?

She stepped out of her rental car, smoothed her pale-blue sundress, took a deep breath and walked into Donny's Diner. It was exactly like she remembered... a small town diner straight out of the old Western movies. Blue and white checkered curtains hung from windows that displayed the daily special neatly written with window paint. Bright red booths—the ones that always made unflattering squeaky sounds when you scooted in—lined each wall.

In front of the kitchen was a bar, lined with red barstools. Behind the counter were three busy waitresses she didn't recognize. The smell of fresh coffee, bread and grease hit her nose as she pushed through the glass door.

Brit waved from the corner booth.

"Hey, girl." Katie slid into the booth and smirked at the unflattering noise.

With a chuckle, Brit said, "Never gets old."

A waitress with bright silver hair and glasses barely holding onto the tip of her nose, walked up to the table. "Howdy ladies, hot as hell out there already, ain't it?"

"Hotter than a two-dollar pistol, Mrs. Booth."

"Well, hey Brit!"

"Hi Mrs. Booth, hey, you remember Katie Somers, don't you?"

"Well I'll be damned! Katie Somers. Is it still Somers?"

"Yes," she smiled, knowing what was about to come next.

"Not married yet? Ah, well, don't fret now, it'll happen. Hey I hear you're a big doctor now."

"Not big, but yes, an archeologist."

"Well good for you. How's your mama?"

"Mom's good, still in England."

Sadness filled the waitress's eyes, "I can't blame her for leaving town after what happened. So sad. I'm so sorry, dear."

"Thanks."

"Well, tell her I said hi, will you?"

"Of course."

"Alright, what can I get for you girls?"

Without looking at the menu, Brit recited her favorite

order. "I'll take the tuna fish sandwich, please, extra mayo and ice tea."

"Alrighty. And for you, Miss Somers?"

"I'll take a turkey wrap and potato chips, please."

"To drink?"

"Iced tea."

"Okey doke. It'll be out soon."

As Mrs. Booth scurried away, Brit leaned forward, placed her hand over Katie's and with a pitiful look said, "Oh, don't worry honey, you'll find some young cowboy to marry you someday."

Katie laughed. "It's not the first time I've had someone pity me for not being married."

Brit puffed her cheeks and leaned back into the booth. "Hell, I ain't yet either."

Katie searched her memory. "I remember you being serious with... Clint back in high school."

"Girl, we were together until just two years ago. Engaged for three years and that bastard would never set the date. Finally, I told him to shit or get off the pot. And sure enough, he got the hell off the pot and we never spoke again."

"Yikes, I'm sorry."

"No, don't be. It's nice being single. I was in a relationship for so long, I didn't realize it, but he had become part of my identity. He was me and I was him. I had no idea what it was like to be on my own... make my own decisions, make mistakes and learn from them. We did absolutely everything together."

Mrs. Booth delivered their iced teas.

Katie shook a Splenda pack, ripped the top off and

poured it into her drink. "That's how my mom and dad were, at least that's what she told me, and then one day he just up and left. She went through the same thing you did, and she turned out to be one hell of a woman."

Brit smiled. "Your mama always was pretty cool. I remember she always brought those delicious fruit platters to the lake."

Katie laughed.

"Hey, that reminds me, you're coming to the Fourth of July party, right?"

"They still do that here?"

"Oh yeah, it's an annual thing, every fourth. The Vonn's still have it in their fancy barn by the lake. Half the town shows up."

Taking a second to respond, Katie sipped her tea, and then said, "I'm planning to leave tomorrow, or the next day, at the latest."

"It's tomorrow night, you have to come!"

Oh, the pressure. Katie looked down and stirred her drink. "Well, if I'm still here, I might."

"No 'might' about it. You're going."

"We'll see."

"That's settled then. You're going." Brit took a sip of her tea. "So, you live in the big city, right? What's it like? I've never been, you know."

As Katie opened her mouth to respond, the front door swung open. She glanced over her shoulder to see Chief McCord and another officer stroll in. She quickly turned back around and sunk down into the booth.

Mrs. Booth delivered an appetizer of warm biscuits,

butter and jelly. As she sat them down, she shook her head in disapproval. "Mmm, mmm, mmm."

Brit looked up. "What are you mmm, mmm, mmm'ing about Mrs. Booth?"

Mrs. Booth leaned in and lowered her voice. "Oh, just McCord over there." She shook her head again. "Strolling in here like he ain't got a care in the world."

Katie sunk a little lower in the seat and avoided eye contact with the waitress.

Sensing gossip like stink on a pig, Brit sat up straight, eyes twinkling. "What do you mean?"

"You ain't heard about the body they found up on Summit Mountain?"

Her eyes widened. "Body? What? Seriously?"

Mrs. Booth waved her hand, "Shhh, child. Yes, last night. They found a woman, dead."

Brit looked at Katie who was aimlessly stirring her tea, then back at Mrs. Booth. "Oh my gosh, no, I can't believe I haven't heard about it. Do they know who it is?"

"Ain't surprised you haven't heard of it yet, the only reason I know is 'cause my daughter-in-law works in dispatch." She glanced over her shoulder. "Rumor has it it's Officer Carl Winters' floozy. That big breasted newscaster."

Brit gasped. "No!" She leaned forward and whispered. "Are you sure?"

Katie was giving her full attention now.

Mrs. Booth nodded. "I probably shouldn't say anything. Ah, hell, it'll be all over the news by tonight anyway, I'm sure." She glanced back at McCord. "And, he's got his little sidekick with him, probably just shootin' the breeze."

"Sidekick? You mean, Officer Danson?"

She nodded. "They're old buddies, went to high school together. McCord was Danson's best man. It's no secret McCord got him a job at the station, and poor Danson just follows him around like a little puppy. Anyway, I'll be back with your lunches in a bit." With that, Mrs. Booth scurried off.

Katie's pulse picked up as she leaned forward and whispered, "So, they know who the girl was? A newscaster?"

Eyes still wide, Brit leaned forward and met Katie's low voice. "I guess... Oh my gosh. Carl's floozy."

"Who's Carl? And what the hell's a floozy?"

"Floozy. Tramp, mistress, you know. How the hell don't you know what a floozy is?"

Not knowing the definition of a floozy was the least of her worries right now. "Alright, alright, give me a break, so who's Carl?"

"Okay, so Carl is a cop. Cute if you ask me, but anyways, rumor had it that he was cheatin' on his wife Suzie. Actually, rumor had it that cheated on him in the past too, but you didn't hear that from me. She's so sweet, poor thing. Anyways, the affair went on awhile without her knowing, but everyone in town knew."

"Everyone knew?"

"Pretty damn much, 'cept poor Suzie. He made a total fool out of her. Bless her heart. So, one night, I guess she finally got her wits about her and got suspicious and followed him. She caught him with his pants down, *literally*, in the back of Amy's car. Rumor has it; Carl's been giving Amy confidential police information so she could have the inside scoop for her news stories. And then, *she* would give *him* the inside scoop... if you know what I mean."

Katie's heart was pounding steady now. Amy. The woman she'd seen less than twenty four hours ago had a name. Amy. She opened her mouth to respond but a knot grabbed her throat.

Mrs. Booth delivered their lunches and Brit quickly took a bite, and then continued the story. "I guess she went nuts, Suzie did. Called up Amy, and threatened the girl and everything." She swallowed and leaned forward. In a low voice, she said, "Two days later, Amy went missing. This was a few days ago. Everyone's been talkin' about it. Carl took time off as soon as the news broke."

Feeling like the wind had been knocked out of her, Katie leaned back.

"And now, she's dead I guess." Brit sipped her tea. "Wow, the gossip is going to be crazy over this one." She looked down at Katie's untouched lunch. "Something wrong with the food?"

"Oh, no, no, sorry… it's just, um, what a sad story." Even though her stomach was rolling, she picked up her turkey wrap and took a bite. "Do they think the wife did it?"

Brit shook her head, "I don't think so, that woman wouldn't hurt a fly."

"Yeah, but you never know what someone's capable of."

"That's true I guess, but, of course when Amy went missing, there were whispers that Carl might've somehow been involved. Regardless if it's him or if it's not…" her eyes narrowed, "looks we've got a murderer running around Berry Springs."

Katie's stomach rolled and she slowly glanced over her shoulder. McCord and Officer Danson had seated themselves at the bar, with their backs to her. At least she could easily slip out without them seeing her.

Anxious to get the hell out, she wolfed down her lunch, listening to Brit fill her in on other gossip. Finally, the bill was paid and they made their way to the exit. The front door swung open.

"Hey, Brit."

"Oh hey, Debbie."

The sun outlined her silhouette as she pushed through the glass doors, and into the diner. Her bleach blonde hair was hot rolled to perfection. She had breasts up to her chin with a face that rivaled any supermodel. A cloud of expensive perfume followed a few seconds after she stepped past them.

Brit rolled her eyes as they stepped outside into the sweltering heat.

"Who was that, and why the eye roll?"

"Oh, that was Debbie. We all call her Diner Debbie around here. Works there. Every man—and boy for that matter—is madly in love with her."

Katie glanced back. Sure enough, every hot blooded male was gawking at her. "Damn, she could be on a Van Halen T-shirt."

Brit snorted. "Well don't go tellin' her that. I'm sure she knows it. Truth is, I think my ex has the hot's for her and has been pursuing her since we broke up."

Katie wrinkled her nose, "I'm sorry."

Brit shrugged and unlocked her car. "Screw him. Come on; let's go to Gardeners for some ice cream."

CHAPTER 11

A SWIFT BREEZE BLEW through his tousled hair as he adjusted the scope, zooming in further. Sweat slicked his skin as the hot sun scorched through the trees. Birds fluttered around him looking for water while squirrels jumped from tree to tree above him, completely unaware of his presence. In full face paint and head-to-toe camo, Jake was almost completely invisible.

High on a mountain top, surrounded by miles of thick woods, he lay on his stomach, pushed up on his elbows, his eye pressed against the long-range spotting scope.

Although he had the black and white print out in his pocket, he'd memorized the quadrants forwards and backwards. He'd read the reports from his supervisor, Mike Woodson, three times, each. He couldn't mess this up. He wouldn't mess this up. It was time to prove himself.

Movement from the west. He shifted his scope to zoom in on the red truck coming down the dirt road. It fit the description. He waited patiently until it veered north, up the driveway to the compound.

Click, Click. He took pictures of the dented, rusty truck.

He followed it up the long, steep driveway to the main house. A man stepped out of the driver's seat. *Click, click.* Another out of the passenger seat—a woman—carrying a shotgun. *Click, click, click.* He didn't recognize her, although he'd analyze the pictures later.

He took more pictures of the men as they unloaded three silver boxes from the bed of the truck and then made their way up to the house. From his vantage point, he could see all fifteen acres of the compound, which consisted of three buildings. One main house, assumed to be the living quarters, and two other large, windowless buildings. The latest intel was that the building farthest from the main house was what was assumed to be the office, where planning, training and target shooting was done. He'd have to confirm that.

The man and woman pushed out of the front door, this time followed by two other men. *Click, click, click.*

The foursome jumped into the truck and drove down to the farthest building. Jake watched as they unlatched the tail gate and unloaded more silver boxes and four large blue barrels. It took two men to carry one barrel. He watched while the boxes and barrels were carefully taken into the building.

Then, nothing.

Sweat dripped off his chin as he waited patiently for more movement.

Seconds faded into minutes, minutes faded into hours. As the time passed he found his thoughts drifting to the previous evening.

After discovering the dead woman in the woods, Jake's first call was to Woodson, to inform him of the news and get his guidance on how to proceed. After a brief exchange, Jake was advised to inform local law enforcement and then assess the situation.

He was undercover, after all.

His thoughts then took a pivot to the other woman he'd found in the woods. Katie Somers. He thought about her long brown hair, her alluring eyes, and her smile.

He'd met a lot of women over the years, but very few actually stayed in his brain the next day. And no women had ever left him daydreaming like he was now. Daydreaming of touching her—her body, her face. Those lips.

There was more to her, no doubt. And he wanted to find out what it was.

Just before he got too worked up, he shook the thought out of his head. A romantic rendezvous was the last thing he needed right now. He had a new job, and he needed to prove himself. All concentration needed to be on the mission at hand, he knew that.

So, why the hell couldn't he stop thinking about her?

He clenched his jaw and forced her out of his head.

A steaming two hours later, he pulled away from the scope, blinked a few times to adjust his vision and wiped the sweat from his brow. Every muscle in his body felt cramped from being still for so long, but that was an all too familiar feeling for him.

He took one last glance through the scope then pushed himself up off the ground. Water. Damn, he needed water. He opened his thermos and gulped ice-cold water for what seemed like a full minute. Then, he packed up his scope and camera, slid on his backpack, slung his rifle over his shoulder and made his way down the mountain. Every muscle screamed at him as he made his way down the steep, treacherous terrain. Instead of wincing at the stiffness, he almost laughed at it. It was nothing compared to what he'd been through in the past, overseas. This was his new life? Where were the bullets whizzing past his head? Where were the helicopters and Humvees? Where were his comrades? This was definitely different, that's for sure.

At the bottom of the mountain, he hopped in his truck, grabbed a backpack from the floorboard and pulled out a clean change of clothes. He felt like a sissy grabbing the baby wipe cloths, but hell, it took off his face paint a hell of a lot better than spit and a towel. He wiped his face and arms clean, then stripped buck naked and pulled on a pair of shorts, a faded Grateful Dead T-shirt and flip-flops. He stuffed his sweat soaked army fatigues into the backpack and glanced in the mirror before turning on the engine. He looked completely different than the man on the mountain. Good. That's exactly what he intended.

He turned on the engine, clicked the air conditioning on high, and a short twenty-five minutes later rolled up the driveway to his mother's house.

"Hi, dear!" Bent over a garden, Nora turned and waved as Shotsky darted across the lawn.

Jake got out of the truck, knelt down and ruffled the dog's ears. "Hey, buddy." He walked up to the budding garden. "Looks great, Mom. It's starting to take shape."

She sat back on her heels and wiped the sweat from her forehead, careful not to transfer dirt from her gloves. "If this damn heat doesn't kill them first. Would you like some tea? Something to eat?"

"No, I'm good, thanks. I'm going to go work on the barn for a bit."

"Alright then, honey." She turned and went back to her work.

He turned to Shotsky. "Stay here with mom, alright?"

Shotsky let out a low whimper before laying down at her feet.

Jake walked around the house, through the backyard to the barn. Before opening the double doors, he glanced over his shoulder to make sure his mother wasn't watching from the windows. He stepped inside, securely closed the door and walked to the stalls.

The barn was like any normal barn; painted red from top to bottom, stalls for the horses, a washroom in the back.

"Hey, buddy."

Butch snorted in acknowledgement. Jake opened the stall door, stepped inside and stroked the horse's long neck. "Why does she have you in here? Maybe taking a break from the sun?" Butch nuzzled into Jake's shoulder. "I'll let you out when I'm done, okay? And maybe we'll go for a ride later."

Another snort and Jake took one last stroke, closed the gate and walked to the corner of the building. He squatted down and pulled away a worn rug to reveal a small trap door, locked. With a touch of his finger, the lock glowed a bright green. He typed in his sixteen digit code and the lock sprung open. Before stepping down the ladder, he looked over his shoulder one last time.

The underground room was about ten-by-fifteen feet—small—but big enough to get the job done. He flicked the switch, illuminating the equipment. Set up like a command center, a black leather chair sat in front of a u-shaped desk lined with computers, surveillance equipment and weapons.

He turned on the secure computer and took a seat. While the center beeped and belched to life, he reached below the desk and pulled an ice-cold Coke out of the mini-fridge. It sizzled as he popped it open. He put on his headset, took a long sip and dialed in.

"Veech, here."

"Veech, it's Thomas."

A second passed while Jakes image connected with Veech's screen at the FBI headquarters. Ethan Veech, a Computer Forensics expert with the FBI, was Jake's main point of contact for all things regarding his mission at hand. Being around the same age, the two had hit it off immediately. Known around the Cyber Crimes Unit just as much for his intelligence as his handsomeness, Ethan was a six-foot-two hunk of chestnut brown hair, dreamy hazel eyes and hard body. Over the last few months Ethan had decided to grow a beard—to his female colleague's dismay—which was beginning to take on a life of its own.

"Hey, bro." Veech squinted and leaned forward to get a better look at Jake's image on his screen. He smirked, "Hey, the seventies called, and they want their shirt back."

Realizing Veech was mocking his favorite Grateful Dead T-shirt, Jake looked down with a solemn expression. "Hey, my dad was wearing this shirt the day he died."

Veech's eyes widened. "Oh. Shit man, sorry."

The corner of Jake's lip turned up. "Just joking, dickhead."

Veech laughed. "Fucker."

"Not lately. Anyway, what you got for me on these anti-government assholes?"

"More communications from their compound, I'm sending them through now." Veech turned away from the screen, typed feverishly and a few beeps later, a transcript lit up on Jake's second monitor. He scanned through as Veech gave him the rundown. "The beginning is more of the usual…"

Jake interrupted, "Are these from the traditional websites and emails they've been communicating through, or anything new?"

"Same ones; the two email accounts, the hunting chat room and Twitter, of course. They're still talking loosely in codes. But, as you know, the communication has picked up in the last few weeks," He shifted back to the transmissions. "So, look toward the bottom on the hunting blog, about half-way down… it looks like they're beginning to stock up on something. *Hunting hogs* over the next few days. Talks about which areas are best, etc."

"Hogs, huh?"

"Yeah—what the hell that's a code word for, I'm not sure. And the hunting spots are codes for a meeting place."

"We need to know who they were communicating to. Did anyone respond directly to their post?"

"Nope."

"What about who's viewed the site?"

"A step ahead of you there. I cross-referenced the IP addresses of who visited the site the day of, and the week following the post, with all the other addresses that visited the site on other days that they posted. And, not surprisingly, the cross-referenced list was as long as my dick."

AMANDA MCKINNEY

"So, just a few addresses then?"

"More like ten thousand; have you seen my girlfriend? Anyway, hunters blog a lot, and this website in particular has a lot of repeat bloggers. Nothing stood out."

"So, you're basically telling me you came up with nothing?"

"Unless you want to convince Woodson to assign a crew to analyze every single one of these IP addresses, I got nothing for you."

Jake blew out a breath. "I might have an idea of what they're stocking up on." Jake plugged his camera into the console. "I'm sending you my pics from today."

"Okay… there, just got 'em."

"Alright. So, Stooge One rolled up to the main house, with an unidentified, at zero-sixteen-hundred. He got the other two Stooges from the house and unloaded a total of eight silver boxes and four blue barrels. I'd bet the silver is ammo, but the barrels are what concerns me."

Veech scrolled through the pictures. "Liquid. It's something liquid."

"Exactly. Looks like thirty-gallon drums to me."

"Yep. They took them right to the office?"

"Yep, two silver boxes went into the house, the rest and the barrels were taken directly inside the office. Click to image thirty-two." He waited a beat for Veech to click on the picture of the female. "I don't recognize her. Run a facial scan."

"Will do, buddy."

"Thanks. We need to figure out what the hell is in those barrels, and more importantly, what it's for."

"Can we assume there's already a target?"

"Other than the Arkansas State Capitol building?"

"That was a fake bomb threat... nothing turned up."

"Yeah, but it doesn't mean that it's still not a future target."

"True. We should be getting the final report on that soon. Do *you* think it's still a target?"

"Not yet. Not enough intel yet, but I'm working on that." Jake clicked his pen angrily against the desk. "We need to see in that damn office. What the hell are they doing with those drums? There's got to be another way to see inside. What about a drone?"

Veech shook his head. "No can do... look, I know this mission is make or break for you, and I'm doing all I can. You know we have limited resources on this one."

"I know." Jake exhaled heavily.

"Well, that's my update. You got anything else?"

Jake nodded and clicked screens. "There was a woman found in the woods yesterday. Gutted. Not pretty."

"No shit?"

He took a sip of his drink. "No shit. I need you to pull the autopsy as soon as it's done."

"No problem. Give me the address and I'll hack in."

"Will do. The local cops are holding this close, I can tell. They knew her personally I think. Something's fishy with this one."

"One of their own?"

"No, I don't think she was a cop. But there's definitely more to this story, internally at least."

"There always is, brother. You need to get out and hear the local gossip."

Jake groaned. "Yeah, there's nothing more I want to do than listen to small town conspiracy theories."

"That's part of being undercover, you know that."

Veech was right and Jake knew it. He needed to become intertwined with the locals. "I'll get out. In the meantime, get me that facial scan ASAP and I'll text you the info for the autopsy."

"Will do."

"Thanks, talk soon."

Jake clicked off the screen and leaned back in his chair. What were these fuckers up to?

Jake's mission was to run surveillance on a notorious anti-government group—who Jake had nicknamed the Three Stooges—who may, or may not have called in a bomb threat at the Arkansas State Capitol building. The information on the group thus far was shoddy, but it was everyone's assumption they were about to take their threats to the next level and begin attacking soft targets. But, who? Why, exactly? That was Jake's job—figure it out, and stay one step ahead of the rednecks, with the help of a single FBI employee, Ethan Veech.

He guzzled the rest of his Coke, then typed his report for the day. After taking one last glance at his email, he turned off each computer, one by one, flicked off the lights, and climbed the ladder up to the barn.

He let Butch out into the field and then made his way to the house.

"I'm making you a ham sandwich," His mother said while spreading mayonnaise on two thick slices of wheat bread, as Jake pushed through the screen door.

He glanced at the clock. "I'll spoil my dinner."

She laughed, well aware that he was mocking how many times she'd said that to him when he was growing up.

"Well, I'm sure you've worked up an appetite with all that work you've been doing in the barn."

He walked over and pecked her on the cheek. "Thanks, Mama."

"Go sit at the table, I'm almost done."

"Yes, ma'am."

Jake sat down, noticing a stack of mail on the table. He picked up the local paper and thumbed through the first few pages. To his surprise, the story of the woman found in the woods hadn't been leaked yet. It would be soon, he had no doubt about that.

"Here you go." Nora set a man-sized ham sandwich, chips and a cold sweet tea in front of him.

"Thanks." He devoured almost half of the sandwich with one bite.

She smiled. "So, have you been around town yet?"

He swallowed the bite and took a gulp of tea. "Other than taking Butch out on the trails, not really."

"Have you even met anyone yet?"

He thought of Katie, but shook his head. "No. And don't get any ideas, Mom. I don't want you setting me up with the first single woman you meet."

"Alright, alright. I'd just like to see you with a nice woman, you know. Southern women are good women." She took a sip of her tea as he ignored her comment. "How's your back?"

"Good."

She eyed him suspiciously, then nodded and said, "Perfect."

He cocked his head. "Perfect?"

"Yep. You can escort me to the Fourth of July party tomorrow night."

He set down his sandwich. "A party?"

"Yep. I befriended our neighbor down the road, and she invited me to it. It's an annual party and the whole town goes. It's supposed to be a big deal." Her eyes lit up. "Dancing, drinks, fireworks."

Dread knotted in his stomach. He knew she'd make him dance with her, just like she did at his middle school dances, and he hated dancing. On the other hand, it could be the perfect opportunity to get to know the locals.

He took a deep breath. "Well, it'd be an honor to escort you, Mrs. Thomas."

She laughed and put her hand over his. "Thanks, sweetheart. Now, finish that sandwich. I need your help in the garden."

CHAPTER 12

"Before we get to your top headlines of the day, we have some breaking news…"

MCCORD TORE HIS eyes away from the computer screen and looked up at the small television in the corner of his office. In bright red letters, the banner *Breaking News, Developing Story* ran across the bottom of the screen.

"… the body of a young woman was found on Summit Mountain early yesterday evening." He reached for the remote—spilling his coffee in the process—and turned up the volume. *"Our sources say a woman and man were hiking on the trails when they discovered the body. The police were on scene within an hour of the discovery. No word yet on the identity, however, as most of you are aware, our own Amy Dunken, a journalist with NAR News, has been missing for over two days now. We are following this story closely and will inform you of any new developments. This is Lanie Peabody, NAR news."*

"Dammit!" McCord pushed out of his chair, grabbed a handful of used napkins out of the trashcan, and began wiping his pants as the door swung open.

"Son-of-a-bitch." Eric Jameson briskly stepped into the small office and took a seat, ignoring the chief's disposition. "You just see the lunch news?"

McCord finished wiping himself down and glared at the unannounced visitor. Jameson was as energetic, alert and sharply dressed as always. The man always seemed to be on point whether it was five in the morning, or ten at night, while the chief was always running to catch up, it seemed. Or, wiping old coffee off of his pants. "Yeah. Yeah, I did."

"Honestly, I'm surprised it took them that long to get wind of it."

He balled up the napkins and threw them in the trash. "That damn Lanie. I thought she was bluffing. She started calling here about an hour ago. Left me three voicemails."

"Me too. Two voicemails. Well, at least she missed the morning papers. It could have been worse."

"Agreed." McCord blew out a breath and sank into his chair. "This thing is only going to blow up more. It's only a matter of time before they link Carl's time off to Amy, assuming it is her, of course." He leaned back in his chair and glanced at the clock. It hadn't even been twenty-four hours since they'd found the body, for Christ's sake. "Have we located her car?"

"Not yet. I've got Walker on it."

"We need to get a confirmed identity."

"I've already pinged Jessica on her cell a few times.

She's either screening me, or knee deep in a body already. Knowing her, I assume the latter."

"Good, keep at it. She knows this is her number one priority. We need to confirm if it's Amy, or not, ASAP." He narrowed his eyes. "And, I mean *ASAP*."

"Amy's dental records have already been sent over. So, Jessica has everything she needs."

McCord nodded.

"You speak with Carl?"

He looked down. "Yeah, last night."

A moment of silence weighed down the room.

"How'd he take it?"

"About as you'd assume. I told him we'd call him as soon as we got a positive ID."

"You *do* think it's her, right?"

McCord looked up, his eyes cold as ice. "Yes."

Jameson nodded. "Me too. Let's hope Carl has a hell of an alibi. You going to bring him in for questioning?"

"One step at a time, Jameson. We take this one step at a time, starting with her ID. If it is Amy, we'll talk to him. Until then, innocent until proven guilty."

Jameson nodded.

"We'll also want to confirm Suzie's alibi for the night of the murder."

Jameson raised his eyebrows, "His wife? Little Suzie? You're kidding."

McCord shook his head. "Nope. She had just found out about the affair, and went nuts from what I heard."

"Come on, McCord, there's no way in hell Suzie did it."

"We'll see."

Annoyed, Jameson pushed himself out of the chair.

"Okay. I've got Jonas working on the cast of the shoeprint now. Will update you as soon as I get the report."

As Jameson turned to walk out, Jonas knocked on the open door. "Good, you're both here."

Barely thirty and smart as a whip, Jonas was the station's go-to guy for research, admin work, or anything else that needed to be done. He took a seat across from the Chief. "No hit yet on the symbol burned into the skin, but I'm still searching."

"Okay, keep at it."

"Also, I scanned Amy Duncan's credit cards and phone records." Jonas handed Jameson a piece of paper. "Her last credit transaction was at Smarty's gas station, at eleven in the morning, the day before her estimated death. I viewed the security camera, she was alone and nothing looked out of the ordinary."

"Okay, so that tells me nothing."

He handed him another piece of paper. "This might. Her last cell phone communication was to none other than Officer Carl Winter's cell phone. June twenty-ninth at ten-twenty in the evening."

McCord closed his eyes and felt the burn of Jameson's and Jonas's stares. Under his breath, he muttered, *"Dammit."* He opened his eyes and leaned forward. "We need to find her car. Get on it."

"Yes, sir." Jonas turned on his heel and left the room.

"What about Lanie?"

McCord stood. "I'll handle her."

Jameson nodded and stepped out of the office.

McCord ran his fingers through his hair and leaned

back in his chair. This was getting messier by the minute, and it was beginning to drudge up old memories.

It had been just over a year since he'd seen another beautiful, young woman dead on the same mountain.

A knot formed in his throat.

Before he could stop himself, he pulled open the bottom drawer of his desk and retrieved a file. He glanced at the door before opening it. His hands began to tremble as he rifled through various papers and pulled out a picture.

A picture of her. Her beautiful smiling face, her curly blonde hair.

He inhaled deeply. He'd never forget that day.

He was instantly pulled back to reality by the beeping alert of a new email. With an exhale, he tucked the picture back in the folder, placed it in the back of the drawer and snapped it shut.

The phone rang.

"McCord here."

"McCord, it's Jessica."

"Is the autopsy done?"

"No, not yet, close, but I confirmed the identity via the dental records."

His stomach dropped. "Okay…"

Pause. "It's her."

He held his breath.

"Amy Duncan."

He squeezed his eyes shut and felt the twinge of a headache brewing. "Okay. Time of death?"

"As I suspected, she had been dead for about thirty-five hours when we found her. The humidity and heat drastically sped up the decomposition process."

"Signs of struggle?"

"Yes, ripped finger nails and bruising. No traceable DNA under the nails."

"Look again."

"I'm pretty thorough, McCord." She didn't bother to hide the annoyance in her voice. "The burned symbol into her skin—it was also done close to the time of her death."

"Have you seen that symbol before? Anywhere?"

"No, not that I can recall."

"Not on any bodies you've seen, even over the years?"

"No."

"Hmm…"

"There's one more thing."

"Yes?"

"She had been… penetrated very close to the time of her death."

McCord tensed, dreading to hear what was next.

"There are traces of DNA that we are going to run an identity on. I… just wanted to give you a heads up on that."

"Jessica, listen to me."

"Yes?"

"Keep those results close, you understand? Call me immediately when you get them, and keep it to yourself."

"Of course."

"And Jessica? Get the whole autopsy done immediately."

"Workin' on it."

Click.

He hung up the phone, minimized his email and clicked on the file he'd saved directly to his desktop named *Amy*. Scrolling down, he opened the picture of the symbol that was burned into her skin. He squinted and leaned forward. No, he didn't recognize it. And he was sure as hell that Carl wouldn't either.

Frustrated, he blew out an exhale. It was now confirmed that the woman was, indeed, Officer Carl Winters' mistress, and it would soon be confirmed that he had been intimate with her the day she was killed. He clenched his jaw. One of his own would be brought in for questioning, for killing the woman he was having an affair with.

That can't happen. Not on his watch.

He picked up the phone.

"Walker here."

"Walker, what information you got on Jake Thomas?"

"I called my Army contact and he confirmed that Mr. Thomas was an Army Ranger as he stated."

"Was?"

"That's right. Was. As in, past tense."

"Well why the hell did he leave? Or get dismissed?"

"They wouldn't tell me."

"Hmm."

"He's also clean as a whistle. No record or anything."

"Okay, what about shoe size?"

"Undetermined right now. Jonas is pulling Mr. Thomas's height and weight from the DMV database. We can get an estimate shoe size based on that information."

"Let me know immediately."

"Yes, sir."

"And Walker? Check out Katie Somers too."

"Yes, sir."

CHAPTER 13

WEARING NOTHING BUT torn jeans, boots and a workman's belt, Jake hammered the last nail into the plank. Twenty down, ten million to go. He straightened and beads of sweat rolled down his tanned, muscular back, wetting the band of his jeans. Although he had opened all the windows and doors in the barn, the Arkansas humidity was still stifling.

Dusk was less than a few hours away and after a long afternoon of manual labor, he wanted nothing more than an ice-cold beer and a porch swing, swaying in the evening breeze. But, he had a few more things to get done first.

Damn this southern heat, he thought, as he sat back on his heels and reached for his water. He was up high in the loft, tackling the most difficult planks first and from that vantage point he could see all the work he still had ahead of him.

Splashing some ice-cold water on his neck and shoulders, he decided it was a good time for a break.

Jake laid down his hammer and glanced at his cell phone, which had one new text message from Veech.

Official report re: AR Capitol bldg just sent.

He climbed down the ladder, made his way to the far corner and squatted down next to the worn rug. Taking a quick glance over his shoulder, he pulled back the rug, plugged in his security code and climbed down into his command center.

The cool air instantly chilled the sweat on his body. No need for air-conditioning this deep in the ground.

He flicked on each system when the phone rang.

"Thomas."

"Yo, Veech here." Veech's bearded face popped up on the monitor and he immediately wrinkled his nose at Jakes bare, sweaty chest. "Shit man, I know we said casual but this is pushing it."

Jake smirked. "Sorry, your mom just left."

He laughed, ignored the quip and clicked a few keys on his computer. "You read the report yet?"

"Just scrolling through it now. Why don't you give me the Cliff notes?"

"Well your name is mentioned."

"Yeah?"

"Well, not your actual name, but it states that an "additional resource" had been assigned to further monitor activity."

"Gotta start somewhere I guess."

"Exactly. So, the report doesn't tell us too much more than what we already know. The call was placed to the main line at the Arkansas Capitol building. Dude in a low muffled voice told the receptionist that 'Today was the beginning, a bomb had been placed somewhere in the building, and that there were more to come'."

"Tell me they traced the number?"

"Nope, it was a burner phone, untraceable. Probably tossed in some trash can in God knows where. But, get this, new information is that the security cameras picked up a white male wearing long sleeves and pants, which is way too hot for the weather, about the same build and size as Stooge One. He had a hat on too, pulled low."

"When?"

"A day before the call was placed. It's not much, you know, but it's something."

"Shit man, we need a hell of a lot more than that to connect the Stooges to the Capitol building threat. What was he doing in the building?"

"That's what seemed out of the ordinary, besides his attire of course. He literally walked in, walked straight to the lobby bathroom, and then walked back out thirty-three minutes later."

"So, the guy went into the Capitol building to take a thirty-three minute piss?"

"Yep."

"Security didn't notice?"

"No, can't really blame 'em."

Processing the information, Jake tapped his pencil. "Okay, then what?"

"After the call, the SWAT team searched the whole building and came up with jack shit."

"So really, this could have just been some twenty-some-thing-year-old prankster. And maybe the dude who walked into the bathroom just had a bad lunch."

"Yeah, but it's interesting information."

Jake snorted. He was used to getting detailed, actionable intel. Not bullshit reports that probably took some big dick's assistant two days to type up. "Well, speaking of interesting, have you checked on the autopsy for the body I found in the woods yet?"

"Yeah, about an hour ago, it's not done yet, or at least, not logged."

He hesitated. "Okay, keep at it. I have no doubt the chief of police is pushing it through. Media's already picked it up."

"Shocker. Stay on it."

"Thanks, buddy. Let me know if communications at the compound pick up. Will report in after surveillance tomorrow."

"Sounds good, man. Have a good one." Veech's face disappeared from the screen.

He minimized his email and brought up his browser. Still open was the local news' webpage with the biggest story scrolling across the front page.

Woman's body found on Summit Mountain …

He leaned back in his chair and tapped his pencil.

Katie Somers.

Something in his gut told him there was more to her than meets the eye. Something needed to dig into, explore. What was she doing on the cliff, alone? Was it a coincidence that a dead body lay less than a hundred yards from her? Yes, his gut was telling him something was there.

Before he could stop himself, he opened a classified, encrypted search engine and typed in Katie Somers.

Thirty minutes later Jake glanced at the clock. "Dammit." He pushed himself out of the black leather chair, turned off the equipment and scurried up to the barn. He had just pulled the rug over the lock, when he heard the barn door opening.

"*Phew*, it's hot in here!" Nora met him in the middle of the barn, carrying a sweating glass of ice tea.

"Better than in the sun. Thanks, Mom."

"Well, I came out here to make sure you remembered our date tonight at the annual Fourth of July party."

He smiled, "How could I forget?"

"Good." She looked up at the rafters and put her hands on her hips. "Looks good, but we've got a hell of a lot more work to do, don't we?"

He nodded. "Yep, this barn needs a lot of work."

Worry lines appeared on her face. "Don't overdo it now. How's your back?"

"Good, Mom. It's fine. Don't worry."

She studied him for a good minute. "Okay, then. Well, I plan on finding some strapping young man to pick up where you leave off, when you leave."

"Make sure I meet him first."

She laughed. "I can take care of myself, you know."

He wrapped his arms around her shoulder. "What are sons for then?"

She pulled up on her tip toes and pecked his cheek. "We leave in thirty minutes, so get that sweaty behind in the shower."

"Yes, ma'am."

❦

Katie stood in front of the long mirror, biting her lip. She smoothed her green jersey dress and adjusted her strapless bra. Thanks to the unrelenting heat, her brown hair was pulled back in a tight ponytail, off her neck and shoulders. She wore light makeup—it would probably sweat off anyway.

Doing a quick spin, she checked herself from all angles.

On second thought, she applied a little red lip gloss. Red lips never hurt anyone.

She took one last look in the mirror. Why the hell was she so nervous? Should she just cancel?

Ding.

Startled, she almost dropped her lip gloss.

Ding.

As she reached for the phone, she noticed her hand was trembling. She turned it on to see a text from Brit.

Fixin to leave. You?

She typed a response. *Yes. See you there.*

She glanced at the clock. It was time to go.

Taking a look around the room, her eyes landed on the open window. Her stomach tickled and she suddenly felt that feeling she'd felt more than once lately... that someone was watching her. She squared her shoulders, walked over and slammed it shut, locking both locks one by one and sending a menacing glare into the darkening woods outside. Yeah, that'll do it.

She slipped on her flip-flops, grabbed her purse and walked through the house closing and locking each window.

"It's going to be hot as hell in here when I get back," she muttered as she turned off each light.

She hesitated at the front door, feeling a pull to stay home. No. She rolled her eyes at herself before stepping out onto the porch, locking the door behind her and jumping into her rental car.

Twenty-minutes later, Katie drove down the long gravel driveway to the Vonn's lake house. Loud country music and laughter floated through the air as she weaved in and out of cars trying to find a parking spot in the field. The whole town really was there.

She maneuvered into a tight spot in between two trees, glanced at her reflection in the rearview mirror and got out of the car.

"Hey girl!"

Katie shaded her eyes from the setting sun. "Hey!"

Brit bounced over in a short, tight floral dress, cowboy hat and flip-flops. "I love your dress!" She reached forward, feeling the jersey fabric.

"Thanks. You were right, there are a lot of people here."

"I know, isn't it great? You've never been to the barn, right?"

"No, I don't think it was built before I left town."

"Oh man, you're going to love it, it's beautiful, come on."

Brit pulled Katie's arm through the field and onto the manicured path leading down to the barn by the river. Her nerves picked up with each step.

Brit inhaled deeply. "Mmm, smell that? They've fired up the grill. Steaks, hamburgers, crawfish, the works."

It smelled heavenly.

The path through the woods took a steep decline before

opening up to an expansive clearing. Katie's eyes widened as she took it all in. At least a hundred people—women dressed in summer dresses and men in jeans and cowboy hats—mingled around covered picnic tables and chairs. Large decorative lanterns hung from the trees, swaying in the evening breeze. In the middle of the clearing stood a large red barn, doors opened wide to display at least four tables filled with food and drinks. Numerous strands of lights hung from the ceiling illuminating a dance floor in the center. A local band played classic country music on a small stage in the back.

Just beyond the barn was the river, sparkling in the setting sun. Bright colors of red, orange and yellow reflected off the water. A few kids splashed in the lukewarm water as their mothers yelled at them for getting their clothes wet.

"Wow, it's beautiful."

"I know, I think they inherited a bunch of money. Anyways, let's get a drink." Brit led the way to the bar, which was set-up outside the barn. They marveled at the fancy selection of wine, liquor and beer.

Dressed in a cowboy hat and pearl snap shirt, the handsome bartender smiled. "What can I get for you ladies?"

"Hey Randy, you remember Katie?"

He cocked his head. "Somers? You look a lot like your mama."

Katie smiled. "Thank you. I don't think we've met."

"Don't think so."

"It's nice to meet you."

"You too, darlin'." He turned toward Brit. "What can I get for ya?"

Brit wrinkled her nose and rubbed her hands together

as if she were making the biggest decision of her life. "Um, gimme a Jack and Coke." A mischievous smile spread across her face. "And make it a double."

"You got it. And for you, ma'am?"

"I'll take a beer, please."

"Yes, ma'am."

Katie took a moment to scan the faces in the crowd, praying that she didn't see Chief McCord.

"Here you go, ladies."

"Thanks Randy." Brit took a sip. "Whew, nice drink!"

Katie laughed and sipped her ice-cold beer. "Let's check out the food."

They made their way into the barn and straight to the hamburger station. Katie's stomach grumbled as she piled her plate with the greasy food.

"No one's dancing yet." Brit scanned the crowd as they took a seat at a small table in the corner. "Give it a few hours… and a few more drinks, this place'll be packed."

With a mouth full of food, Katie shook her head, "Not me. You know I don't dance."

"Please. Everyone dances at this party. It's a must."

Katie was about to protest again when she saw Chief McCord, Officer Walker and Detective Jameson step into the barn, causing her to choke on her half-chewed bite of hamburger.

"You alright, Katie?" Brit slammed her on the back.

"Yeah, ouch, stop. Yeah, I'm fine."

"Damn girl, try chewing first."

Katie nodded and took a sip of her beer, eyeing the chief over the rim.

She pretended to be listening to Brit chatter something about a new pair of shoes, as she nibbled on a fry and watched McCord from across the barn. He was dressed in casual clothes—wrangler jeans, a red button-up and a cowboy hat. He made small talk with a few people then made his way across the barn. Jameson and Walker had broken away from him and were already piling BBQ ribs onto large plates.

She watched McCord make his rounds, then start to make his exit. He was almost outside when he turned and looked directly at Katie. Her stomach dropped.

Eyes narrowed, he turned in her direction but was intercepted by a group of men.

Katie exhaled a sigh of relief. A run in with McCord was the last thing she needed.

Brit drained the rest of her drink and glanced at Katie's empty beer. "Come on, let's get another drink."

After tossing her paper plate in the trashcan, she followed Brit to the bar, who busied herself by flirting with the bartender.

Katie gazed out at the river. The sun had just set behind the mountains and the remaining light sparkled off the water like a million diamonds. To the west, stars were just beginning to twinkle.

A light breeze blew through her dress as she turned back toward the crowd, and then she saw him.

CHAPTER 14

HIS BLUE EYES locked on hers, as if there were no one else around.

She stared back, butterflies dancing in her stomach. She hadn't expected to see him tonight.

He was standing across the clearing, the gold glow from the lanterns illuminating his face. He was dressed casually in a T-shirt, jeans and flip-flops and looked even sexier than when she first saw him on the cliff.

His eyes twinkled and she swore she saw a small smile curve on his lips right before someone stepped in front of him, blocking her view.

"Come on, let's mingle." Brit grabbed Katie's arm and led her back into the barn. As she stumbled through the grass, she took one more glance over her shoulder, but Jake was gone.

"Man, can you believe how many people are already here?" Brit guided Katie over to a cluster of covered hay barrels and took a seat.

"No, you weren't kidding about the whole town showing up."

"Miss Somers." Katie turned to see Chief McCord standing behind them, arms crossed over his chest.

Her face flushed with emotion. "Hi, Chief."

"Quite a crowd here tonight."

"Yes."

Completely oblivious, Brit piped up. "You gonna dance later, Chief McCord?"

"Doubtful." He looked back at Katie. "I was wondering if you'd be here tonight."

She glanced at Brit. "She convinced me."

"Ah, I see. I figured you'd still be too upset from what you saw on the mountain."

Brit's head snapped up. "What?" She looked at Katie. "What did you see on the mountain?"

"I'll tell you later."

"What did you see? *Amy*? Oh my gosh, are you the one who found Amy?"

She set her jaw. "Brit, I'll tell you later."

McCord stepped closer. "You know, we never got to finish our conversation that day. You said you had only just met Mr. Thomas?"

She opened her mouth to respond when she saw it. A pearl button missing on his red plaid shirt. A white, pearl button. Her stomach dropped to her feet.

Suddenly, a low, deep voice sounded behind them. "We already gave our statements to Officer Walker. If you have further questions for Miss Somers, now is not the time or the place."

Katie turned to see Jake towering behind them. The soft smile she saw just minutes ago was gone and replaced by a menacing glare directed at McCord.

McCord turned and raised his eyebrows. "Well, if it isn't Jake Thomas." He looked him up and down.

Now realizing she was in the middle of heavy drama, Brit's mouth gaped open.

McCord squared his shoulders. "Mr. Thomas, are you enjoying your *leave*? When do you return to active duty?"

No response.

McCord continued, "I must be confused. Are you currently *in* the Army, or not? Because my sources say you were released."

Silence.

McCord nodded and glanced down at Jake's shoes. But before he could ask the question, Jake quipped, "Size fourteen, McCord. Three sizes larger than the tracks at the scene, in my estimation."

McCord raised his eyebrows and Jake continued, "Thought I'd save you some trouble."

From across the barn, Jameson motioned toward McCord. "*Hey, come here for a second!*"

"Have a nice evening, Chief McCord," Jake said.

McCord gave Jake an icy glare and slid Katie a glance before turning and walking out of the barn.

Mouth still open, Brit was staring up at Jake, practically drooling. "I don't believe we've met."

"Jake Thomas, nice to meet you." He looked at Katie. "Want to go for a walk?"

Brit eagerly responded for Katie. "Yes, yes she wants to go."

"Alright then." Jake extended his hand, pulling Katie off the hay bail.

Her heart was pounding. Was she sure a button was

missing off McCord's shirt? A white, pearl button? Exactly like the one she found on the cliff the day her sister died? She needed to look again. She needed to be sure.

She took a deep breath to steady her breathing and fell into step beside Jake as they made their way past the crowd, to the trail. Katie's mind raced as they walked in silence while Jake led her down to the river.

Night had fallen and twinkling stars filled the dark sky. The usual roar of heat bugs was drowned out by the melody of the babbling river. An old Willie Nelson song echoed faintly from the barn.

"You okay?" They slowed to a stroll, walking along the water.

Before answering, she looked over at him. His tall, thick body towered over hers and the moonlight illuminated his blue eyes, strong jawline and supple lips. Something about him stirred her.

"Yeah, I'm okay." She glanced over her shoulder. "I didn't expect to see you here."

"My mom dragged me."

"I know the feeling. My friend, Brit, did the same."

"Kind of like how she pushed you to come on this walk with me?"

Katie smiled. "She's a pistol."

He cut to the chase. "Was that the first time McCord approached you?"

Her shoulders tensed. "Since that night? Yes."

"Don't let him push you around."

Why was he so protective of her? This wasn't the first time she saw it. She saw it when he took control of the situation after seeing Amy in the woods. She saw it, again, when he stepped in between her and Walker while he was questioning her. She saw it tonight when he interrupted McCord and pulled her away.

She'd told herself a million times that she didn't need a man to take care of her. But something deep inside her wanted it... *from him.* Maybe it was because she was out of her element, being back in Berry Springs. Maybe it was the murder. Maybe it was just him. Maybe not.

"Despite what you might think, I can take care of myself."

He grinned. "Yeah? So, you're just a typical ass-kicking Southern cowgirl, huh?"

"That's right, and don't forget it." She smiled.

They walked a few steps. He slid his hands in his pockets and looked over at her. "I'm sorry about your sister."

She looked up at him. How had he heard about that? "Thanks."

They walked along the dark riverbank in a comfortable silence, with nothing but the babbling water and the sound of the rocks crumbling underneath each footstep.

Finally, Katie asked, "Why did McCord ask if you were active in the Army?"

Silence.

"You said you were an Army Ranger, right?"

He nodded.

"So, you're just out on leave?"

He glanced out at the water, avoiding eye contact.

"Why were you carrying a gun that day?"

With this question, he laughed. "Did it make you uncomfortable, Katie? Can't handle a man with a gun?"

"No... it just surprised me is all."

He stopped, turned and faced her. Her heart fluttered as he took a step closer, and something sparked in his eyes as he looked down at her. He stepped even closer. She could almost feel his breath on her skin. For a moment, she thought he might kiss her. Butterflies danced in her stomach with anticipation as she looked up at him.

Kiss me.

Her heart a steady hammer in her chest.

Kiss me.

His lips slowly parted, and as if a magnet pulled her to him, she leaned forward, her weight on her tip toes. He leaned in and just as she closed her eyes...

"Hey Katie!" Brit's voice yelled down from the hill, shattering the moment between them.

Katie's eyes darted open, and completely engulfed in embarrassment now, she tore her eyes away from his, took a step back and turned toward her friend. Her voice cracked as she said, "Be right there." She turned back toward Jake, who had taken a step back as well. His eyes, intense, gazed into hers.

Her cheeks, which were already flushed, turned a deeper shade of red.

"I guess I need to get back."

He hesitated. "I guess I'll walk you then."

As they turned back toward the barn her heart fluttered. They'd almost kissed. He almost kissed her. She felt like a school girl, filled with excitement and longing. Giddy. It was that exciting feeling that once you felt it, it was like a drug that you want again and again. The kind of feeling that throws you off your game, in the most wonderful way. Butterflies. Yep, true butterflies. It had been years since she'd felt her head and heart floating through the clouds like she did now. And, it was at that moment, that she knew she was going to want to feel it again, and again, and again.

She had no doubt that her cheeks were still pink as they stepped up to the clearing where Brit was now gathered in a small group.

"Hey Katie!" Sipping beers and dressed in jeans and cowboy hats, Greg and Paul had made it to the party.

"Hey Greg, Paul. How are you guys?"

Paul cocked his head and looked Jake up and down. "Who's this?"

"This is Jake."

They shook hands.

Jake stiffened as Greg squeezed his arm around Katie and said, "So glad you made it. It's good to see you getting back in the swing of things."

"Thanks, it's a hell of a party."

"I was just telling Brit that a group of us are going camping tomorrow. Interested?"

"Where ya'll going?"

"Out on my dad's land."

Paul laughed, "Greg's set himself up a lair out there."

"A lair?"

"Hey, a man needs a man cave."

"The cave part isn't supposed to be literal, dude."

"The cave makes it all the more fun." He winked at Katie. "Besides, I grew up in these woods, they're like my home anyways. And every man needs a place to go to think."

Brit looked at Katie. "Wanna go?"

"It sounds like fun, but I've still got a lot of unpacking to do."

Greg shrugged. "Suit yourself." He looked down at his drink and turned to Paul, "I'm empty. Let's head to the bar." He looked back at Katie and winked. "Save me a dance."

As they turned and walked away, Katie's gaze landed across the field and her spine stiffened with a blast from the past. A nightmare from the past.

"I'll be right back." Without waiting for Jake and Brit's response, Katie pushed past them and made a bee-line across the field.

With every step, memories leapt into her head. Memories of her sister, of family dinners, and the wedding.

She hadn't seen him since the funeral, but he looked mostly the same, except a bit more rough around the edges, and twenty pounds lighter. His blonde hair was longer than she remembered, and the handsome, lively face was now replaced with the onset of wrinkles and dark circles. He wore a wrinkled shirt, faded Levi's and flip-flips.

His gazed landed on her and for a split-second she thought he was going to turn around and run.

"Zach."

Almost breathless, he replied, "Katie."

For a moment, they said nothing.

"I didn't expect to see you here."

"I'm in town for just a few days… to sell the house, actually."

His expression clouded, the surprise of seeing her was replaced with sadness and pain. He glanced toward the woods. "Take a walk with me?"

She nodded.

She and her sister's ex-husband broke away from the crowd and headed toward the trail. As the music and laughter began to fade, she realized that she had no idea what to say to him. Accuse him of murdering her sister? Or, tell him she's sorry for all the accusations? Or...

"How have you been? How's your mom?"

"Good, I guess. She's... mom left town, I'm assuming you heard that."

He nodded and shoved his hands in his pockets.

"How have you been, Zach?"

A minute ticked by, and with an inhale, he shook his head, and she realized he was doing his best to hold back tears.

She halted, and turned toward him. The dim light of the trail lanterns reflected in his watery eyes. "Zach?"

And with that, the tears fell from his eyes.

"Katie... I..."

Her muscles tensed with anticipation for what he was about to say. He took a shaky, deep breath to compose himself.

"Katie, I'm so sorry."

"For what?"

"Just for everything. I'm sorry that I didn't contact you after Jenna died, and I'm sorry for everything I did in the past, for being an unfaithful little shit to your sister. She didn't deserve it, and I didn't deserve her."

Katie put her hand on his shoulder. "It's okay, Zach. Thank you for saying that."

"Look, I know... I know the gossip." He laughed, a humorless laugh, and shook his head, "Which is exactly why I don't leave my damn house anymore. My buddy dragged me here tonight. But, I just need to hear from you that… that you don't think I had anything to do with it."

She inhaled to speak, but her words caught.

He continued. "I don't blame everyone for thinking it. Always look at the disgruntled ex-husband, right? But, you know that McCord raked me over the coals, don't you? He interviewed each of my alibis, and reviewed the surveillance cameras at my work over and over again. I had no part in it."

"Well, according to McCord, she slipped and fell anyway. No one had a hand in it."

His head snapped up. "Bullshit. *Bullshit*, Katie. She grew up on that damn cliff. You and I both know she didn't slip and fall."

From the trailhead, drunken laughter dissolved what little privacy they had.

She had no idea what to say. Even Zach didn't believe Jenna had fallen.

Zach looked down and whispered, "I have a lot of regrets in my life, but most of them involve Jenna. I just wanted you to know that, and know how sorry I am for causing her pain."

Katie nodded. "Let's get back to the party."

He leaned in for a hug and after they parted ways, Katie had a feeling she'd never see Zach again.

Feeling like an ounce of the weight from the past had been lifted off of her, Katie walked into the barn. The band was roaring and the dance floor was filled. Laughter echoed off the walls. Across the large room, she spotted Brit who had cornered Jake, undoubtedly trying to learn more about the new guy in town.

Jake saw her immediately, and smiled.

"Thought I'd lost you."

She smiled back. "Only temporarily."

Brit grabbed Katie's beer and took a swig. "Where'd you go?"

"Just for a quick walk."

"Well, I need another drink. I'll leave you two alone." With a wink, Brit sauntered off.

"My baby!" Jake and Katie turned to see Jake's mom walking over, her curious eyes locked on Katie. "And, who's this young lady?"

"Mom, this is Katie Somers."

"It's a pleasure to meet you." Katie stretched out her hand but was denied when Nora came in for a hug. "You're a beautiful thing, aren't you?"

Katie flushed, for what seemed like the tenth time.

"Now, where did you two meet?"

"On the cliff a few days ago, not too far from the house."

"That's lovely," she turned to Katie, "You live here?"

"No, I live in New York, but I grew up here."

"It's a beautiful little town."

"Yes, ma'am, it is."

Smiling, Nora looked up at her son. "Jake, you promised me a dance, but only after you take this young lady for a spin."

He wrinkled his nose and did his best to mute the low groan in his throat.

"Oh, come on!" She pushed Jake and Katie onto the dance floor. "Go, go!"

"I'm sorry," Jake said as he slid one hand on Katie's waist and held her hand with the other.

Katie smiled. "It's okay; I'm not a big dancer either." She stepped into him as the band began playing the slow country tune of Strawberry Wine.

Inches apart, she followed his lead as they swayed back and forth with the music. It seemed they picked up right where they'd left off at the river.

The warm glow of the string lights twinkled in his eyes as he looked down at her. The electricity between them prickled her skin as his hand slid lower on her hip.

His strong arms guided her across the dance floor as she gazed into his eyes.

For a moment, nothing else mattered. No one else was in the room. The sounds were drowned out by her own heart beating passionately in her chest.

He tightened his grip on her hand as she leaned closer into him. Heat radiated off of his hard body, perfuming the air of fresh soap, and the indescribable smell of a man. A strong man. Her heart beat faster.

She found herself lost in him. In everything about him. Not just his smoldering sexiness, but in the way she felt when she looked at him.

With a soft smile on her lips, she began to close her eyes when she felt his arms stiffen. She looked up, his expression suddenly pulled tight with intensity. Following his gaze, she looked over her shoulder to see McCord on his cell phone less than ten-feet away. She strained to hear.

"*Three forty-one County Road 24… She's sure it was gun-shots? Okay, we're on our way.*" McCord yelled over to Walker and the two of them briskly walked out of the barn doors.

Jake released his grip, and looked down at Katie. "That's my mom's land."

He grabbed her hand, pulled her off the dance floor and walked over to Nora. "Mama, I've got to go do something real quick. You stay here and have fun, okay? I'll call you soon."

Concern washed over her face. "Is everything okay?"

"Yes, have fun, see you soon."

He grabbed Katie's hand and led her outside. "You got a car?"

She nodded.

They jogged up the steep trail to the parking area. After weaving through the cars, he stepped up to her blue rental and extended his open palm, for the keys.

She tossed him the key ring. "How the hell did you know what car I drove?"

"Lucky guess." He unlocked the passenger door, and reached out his hand. "Get in."

Looking up at him, she hesitated for a moment. Should she stay? Should she go?

He cocked an eyebrow, giving her an are-you-in, or, are-you-out glance. She inhaled deeply, and then clasped his hand as he helped her into the car.

Yes, she was in.

The car creaked and groaned as they flew over the bumpy dirt road.

Anticipation mixed with apprehension crept up as she watched the trees zooming past the passenger side window. The full moon cast a spooky blue glow across the dirt road and black shadows stretched like skeleton fingers from the trees. The night had an eerie feeling; as if something evil was lurking in the mountain.

Less than thirty minutes ago, she and Jake were strolling by the river, underneath a sky full of twinkling stars. Less than thirty minutes ago, she swore Jake Thomas almost kissed her. Now they were barreling down County Road 24, responding to shots fired.

In the distance she could hear the wails of the sirens. "We're getting close."

Jake exited the main road, veering left onto a narrow road with only tire ruts marking a path.

Katie narrowed her eyes and looked at him. "Being down here for just a few days, you sure seem to know the backroads pretty well."

He looked over at her. "You don't trust me?"

She looked forward.

"I make it a habit to make sure my mom is safe, wherever she is, so I studied the land."

They bounced around a corner, where just fifty-yards ahead were two police cars. Jake hit the brakes. "That must be the spot."

"Why are you stopping here?"

He glanced in the rearview mirror and punched the car in reverse. "We're close to my mom's house. We'll park there and take Butch out."

"Jake, maybe we shouldn't go. The cops have it covered." She began regretting her decision to ride shotgun.

He slid onto the main road and cut her a glance. "Do they? This is my mom's land. You're damn sure I'm going to check it out. You don't have to go."

He slammed the car into drive and a short few minutes later, pulled up to the large log cabin home.

"Wow, this is beautiful."

"It's too much for her to keep up if you ask me."

He hopped out of the car and opened Katie's door. "Let's go."

She had to jog to keep up with his long strides as they walked down the path that led to the barn. "Is all this land hers?"

He pulled open the barn door. "Yeah."

Butch snorted with excitement as Jake pulled him from the stall and saddled him up. With one swift move, he lifted Katie onto the saddle and jumped in front of her.

"Hold on to me."

As they made their way through the dark field, she looked up at the full moon and shivered. A feeling of foreboding washed over her—her sixth sense. She took a deep breath and tried to shake the negative thoughts from her head. The shots heard were probably just some late night hunters. That's probably all it was.

Jake hesitated at the woods' tree line and turned to her. "Whatever happens, I don't want you to get off Butch. If we get separated, ride Butch back to the barn." He reached in his pocket and tossed her a compass. "Go southeast until you hit the fields, then you should see the barn."

Her pulse quickened. Why would they get separated? What was he expecting to find?

She nodded and took the compass as Butch pressed into the darkness.

She'd only been in the woods after nightfall a few times as a kid and it was just as creepy now, if not more than it was then.

The thrum of bugs filled the air, along with occasional screams from whatever critter was on the hunt, or being hunted.

They walked for what seemed like twenty minutes, when Jake pulled the reigns for Butch to stop. A low growl rumbled through the woods.

Jake reached down and pulled out his Glock.

"Don't move," he whispered to her.

Another growl, this time louder. They turned toward the sound, where the moonlight illuminated a large log surrounded by a thick bush.

The bush rustled with movement.

Katie's heart began to pound.

Keeping his eyes on the fallen tree trunk, Jake reached into the saddlebag and pulled out a flashlight. Hand steady, he flicked it on and aimed it toward the sound.

A silver coyote raised its head from the bush, its beady, black-eyes reflected in the light as it stared back at them.

Strands of flesh hung from the coyote's mouth, blood dripped from its jaw.

A human foot jetted out just past the fallen log.

CHAPTER 15

IN BARELY A whisper, Katie exhaled, "Oh my God," and covered her mouth with her hand.

"Stay here."

Gun in hand, Jake slid off the horse. The coyote snarled, spraying spit and blood from its mouth.

Eyes locked on the animal, Jake slowly bent down, picked up a rock and hurled it through the air. With a yelp, the coyote turned and darted into the woods.

A cold sweat broke out over Katie's body as she watched Jake walk up to the log. She knew. She saw it in his face when he shone the light on the ground.

"Jake?"

His eyes met hers. "Another body."

Sprawled on the dirt, lay a naked man, gutted, with a police badge pinned through his chest. His lifeless eyes stared blankly into the dark sky and just below the two bullet holes in his chest was small symbol, burned into his skin.

"Hands on your head!"

Katie screamed as Chief McCord stepped out of the dark woods, gun aimed at Jake.

"Whoa, whoa." Jake began to raise his hands.

McCord stepped forward. *"Put the gun down!"*

"Okay." His voice calm and cool, Jake bent down and tossed his gun toward McCord.

"Now put your hands on your head and get on your knees."

Jake did as he was told.

Not realizing she had been holding her breath, Katie inhaled as the shock of the scene around her began sinking in. *Say something, you idiot.* Her voice shook as she said, "McCord, calm down, we just got here, we just saw it."

McCord looked at Katie and his face softened minimally. "Katie. Dammit, what are you doing here?"

Just then, Walker darted through the brush, gun drawn. Quickly assessing the situation, he stepped up to Jake and nodded at McCord as if to say 'I got him.' McCord lowered his gun and looked down at the dead body. The blood drained from his face.

"Oh my God… Danson." He turned toward Jake, his face red with rage. "What the hell are you doing here, son? This is the second fucking body you've been standing next to this week."

"This is my mom's land; I have every right to be out here."

"Next to a dead body? Next to a *fellow officer's dead body?"* The veins pulsed in McCord's neck as he stepped up to Jake.

Katie's head began to spin.

"Whoa, McCord." Walker held up a hand. "We literally just saw these two less than twenty minutes ago at the party." He looked down at the body. "This isn't that fresh."

Eyes wild, McCord inhaled deeply and took a few steps back. He reached in his pocket and pulled out a cigarette. "Get everyone the fuck out of here. Immediately."

"Yes, sir." Walker looked at Jake, "Want me to cuff him?"

McCord eyed Jake for a moment, and then gave a quick nod. "And bag his gun."

Katie watched as Walker slapped handcuffs on Jake. Her stomach dropped when he turned toward her. "Want me to cuff her?"

Jake's head snapped up. "No. There's no need to cuff her."

McCord blew out a stream of smoke. "Well, what a fucking gentlemen you are." He took another drag. "You said you were checking on your mom's land?"

Jake nodded.

"Why? Why tonight? Now? At nine at night?"

"I overheard your conversation about shots fired, and recognized the address."

"Maybe you came out here to move the body you dumped."

Jake glared in response.

"Maybe you were worried we'd find it." Pause. "So, you expect me to believe its complete coincidence that you have *found* two dead bodies out here? You just show up in this town out of the blue, and all of a sudden two people are murdered?" He snorted. "Boy, I hope you have a good fucking lawyer."

"Chief McCord, I've been with him each time. It's the truth."

"You need to pick your men better, Miss Somers. And don't worry; you'll have plenty of time to tell your side of the story."

"Team will be here in five." Walked slipped his phone into his pocket.

"Good. Take Mr. Thomas down to the station."

"You have nothing to hold me on."

"The fuck I don't."

"I have an alibi for tonight, and every evening that I've been here." He narrowed his eyes, "And, I do have a good fucking lawyer."

Walker stepped up to McCord and whispered in his ear, "He's right man. Shit, you and I saw him at the party tonight."

"This kid has been in town less than seventy-two hours and is already connected to two bodies. The fuck if I can't haul his ass to jail."

"What about Katie?"

"Formally question her, too."

"Yes, sir."

Walker stepped up to Jake, "Let's go. And Katie, we'll need you down at the station for questioning as well."

Her stomach churned. "Okay…" she looked down at Butch, then at Walker, "what about the horse?"

"Yours?"

"No, Jake's."

"How far away are we from your house?"

"About ten minutes."

"Alright then, take him back and we'll pick you up there."

Jake shook out of Walker's grip. "Bullshit! She's not going through these woods alone right now."

Katie leaned down, "Jake, I'll be fine. I remember. Southeast until the field, then straight to the barn."

Jake clenched his jaw as Walker grabbed his arm and said, "It's settled, let's go."

As Walker pulled Jake through the woods, he glanced over his shoulder, taking one last look at Katie. His lip parted and although he said nothing, she knew.

She nodded. Yes, she'd be careful.

Katie watched Jake fade into the darkness until McCord's agitated voice yanked her back into the nightmare. As he barked orders into his cell phone, Katie pulled Butch's bridal. She leaned down and whispered, "Tsk-tsk, let's go, boy" and with that, she and Butch set off in the direction they had just traveled from.

The night was dark. Darker than it was just thirty-minutes ago.

She kept glancing over her shoulder until the glow from McCord's flashlight faded into the distance. A clatter of voices echoed through the woods, presumably the team making their way to the scene.

Every muscle in her body squeezed with tension as they stepped through the dense brush.

The moonlight shot streams of light through the trees swaying in the breeze.

She closed her eyes to steady her breathing.

"Okay, Butch, we're okay. We just need to get back." She took another nervous glance over her shoulder.

With the compass guiding her, each minute seemed to

last an hour. She calculated they'd been walking for about ten minutes. Shouldn't she see the fields by now?

Her heart skipped a beat when she heard movement just behind her. Goosebumps ran over her body and her fingers gripped the reigns tighter.

More rustling. Louder.

Her heartbeat raced as she leaned down into Butch's ear, "We need to get out of here, buddy." She tapped her heels and he picked up his pace.

Whispers. She swore she heard whispers.

She glanced over her shoulder into the darkness.

Footsteps. Did she just hear footsteps?

Fear gripped her. "Go, boy!" She dug her heels into Butch and flapped the reigns. "*Go!*"

Butch took off in a sprint, tearing through the brush. Twigs and leaves slapped against her legs and arms. Her green dress whipped against her thighs.

Her skin crawled with fear, as if a large hand was reaching for her, closer, closer until it almost had her.

A branch sliced past her leg sending a hot, stinging pain through her body.

Finally, she saw the fields up ahead. "Go, Butch, go!"

Butch leapt through the air and over the fence, bouncing her on the saddle as they landed. She exhaled with relief when she saw the barn in the distance. Thank God she was out of the woods.

As her pulse began to steady, she glanced over her shoulder.

Just beyond the fence line, she swore she saw the dark outline of a man, looking straight at her.

✍

Katie wrapped her arms around herself and looked around. The room was blinding white and mostly bare, the metal chair she sat in as cold as ice. In front of her was a small table with a tape recorder and a Styrofoam cup filled with water that one of the officers had brought her.

This was the second time she'd been in this room. Just last year, she sat at the same table describing the events leading up to her sister's death, and now she was there to describe the events leading up to the *second* dead body she'd seen in less than three days.

The police station was exactly like she remembered. Bleak, gray walls, and the smell of stale coffee lingered in the air.

She didn't belong here.

The station was buzzing with the news that one of their own had been slain. Groups of officers and other personnel huddled in corners, whispering. Others wept. Others silent; grieving in their own way.

No, she didn't belong here.

She closed her eyes and took a deep breath. Whether she wanted to face it or not, one thing was for certain, dead bodies were stacking up all around her. Her sister. Amy Duncan. And now, a police officer, they called Danson.

Her mind drifted to Jake, and she found herself asking the question that had been brewing in her stomach since she'd arrived at the station—was it possible that Jake had something to do with the murders? How well did she really know him? She couldn't ignore the coincidence that he had been the one to find both bodies, with her. Was he a good guy? A bad guy? Mysterious, for sure. And, right now, he was sitting in a jail cell somewhere in the building.

Her stomach curdled at the thought.

She slouched over and clenched her fists. What a mess. What a huge, catastrophic mess she was in.

"Miss Somers."

Her head snapped up to see a tall man in plain clothes enter the room, followed closely by Officer Walker.

"I'm Lieutenant Rubin. May I call you Katie?" They briefly shook hands.

"Yes."

Rubin nodded and sat in the chair across from her. Walker faded into the corner of the room.

He pressed a button on the recorder. "Katie, let me explain the interview process to you. We'll start off by getting some general background information from you, okay?"

Nerves shot through her body. "Yes."

"Great. Then, I'm going to ask you about the evening of July second. I need you to be as detailed as possible in your response, alright?"

She nodded.

"Good. Next, I'll ask you the same type of questions about this evening's events, okay?"

"Okay."

"Great. Can you confirm the spelling of your full name, Katie Anne Somers, please?"

She spelled out each letter of her name.

"Thanks. And your birth date?"

She rattled off her birthday. Officer Rubin proceeded

to ask her general questions such as address, names of relatives, employment, etc. Finally, he dove in.

"Katie, based on your statement on July second, you said that you had just met Jake Thomas for the first time, is that correct?"

"Yes. About thirty-minutes before we found the body."

"Where?"

"On the cliff. I was up there with my horse, looking at the view and he walked up behind me."

"What did he say to you?"

She paused for a minute. "He said hello… and asked if I was alone."

For the first time, Rubin scribbled in his notebook. "And what did you respond?"

"I said, yes."

He scribbled more. "Then, what?"

"He asked if I was from here, I said, yes, again. Then, I asked him the same question, and he told me he was from Montana, and was here helping his mom move in." Katie recited the rest of their conversation.

"So, his dog got jumpy, causing him to venture off into the woods, where you followed?"

"Yes."

"And he went straight up to Amy Duncan's body?"

"Yes, sir."

"Can you please confirm who called for help?"

"He did."

Another scribble in his notebook. Then, he asked Katie to describe the events of the current evening, starting with arriving at the party, which she did.

"Katie, did you get a good look at the gun he carried on both nights?"

"I think so."

"Did they look like the same gun?"

"I think so."

He clicked off the recorder, leaned back in his chair and took a deep breath; his demeanor relaxing. "Miss Somers, Katie, relax. I believe you had nothing to do with this, okay?"

She released the tension cramping her shoulders and exhaled loudly.

"But, don't you think it's ironic that Mr. Thomas shows up and two people are suddenly murdered?"

She opened her mouth to respond, but found herself at a loss for words.

"Katie, I want you to stay away from Jake Thomas. If he reaches out to you, in any way, I want you to call us immediately."

"Officer Rubin," she hesitated, "he didn't murder those people, couldn't have."

"Why so sure, Katie?"

She paused and shook her head. She didn't have a good answer, and he knew it. They sat in silence for a moment.

"Well, you're free to go Miss Somers. We've got a car outside waiting to take you to your car. I'll walk you out."

Officer Rubin led her down the hall and into the main lobby. "Sign out here and, Katie," he stepped closely and whispered, "and, be smart."

Walker held up a phone and motioned for the Lieutenant on the other side of the door.

"Bye, Katie." The door closed behind him.

As Katie completed the paperwork, she overheard Rubin's conversation.

"Lieutenant John Rubin... Yes, Jake Thomas was admitted less than an hour ago..." His voice became agitated, *"... released? But, sir, we have reason to believe he is connected to two murders... I don't give a damn about your credentials..."* There was a long pause and Katie could swear she heard yelling through the phone. Eventually Rubin said, *"Yes sir... I'll release him immediately."*

CHAPTER 16

JAKE JERKED AWAKE the moment the plane landed on the runway. He glanced at his watch. Seven-thirty in the morning.

He sat up and rubbed his eyes. What a hell of a night. He was on less than three hours of sleep, and had already received two calls from Woodson, expressing his disappointment in Jake's judgment. Apparently, it wasn't ideal for undercover agents to get tossed in jail.

At the end of one of the ass chewing's, Woodson had also informed Jake that he would be on the red-eye flight out to DC the next morning. Regardless of Jake's carelessness, a second dead body spun his assignment into overdrive.

So, here he was.

He made his way through the airport, running over his report in his head. He needed to be on his A-game today. No room for error.

"Thomas." Veech met him just off the escalators. His beard had grown at least an inch since Jake had last seen him.

"Damn dude, did they search that thing before letting you into the airport?"

Veech stroked the mess of hair on his chin. "Naw, I can only hide a small box knife at this point, nothing to worry about." An ornery smirk slid across his face. "So, how was the pokey? Meet any eligible bachelors?"

"I'm not in the mood, bro."

They exited the airport and stepped into the parking garage, where Veech's needling continued. "It was that good, huh? You weren't even in there that long."

"Yep, in and out in less than a minute, kinda like your last lay."

Veech laughed, "I'm just giving you shit. Relax, princess."

They jumped in Veech's unmarked Taurus.

Jake leaned his head back on the seat. "What time do the meetings start?"

"Eight-thirty on the dot."

"Okay, lay out the schedule for the day."

Carefully navigating the heavy traffic, Veech prepped Jake for the long day ahead.

What seemed like hours later, they finally pulled up to FBI Headquarters.

Veech glanced at his watch. "We gotta jog, man."

They quickly moved through security and made their way up to the third floor conference room.

"Thomas, Veech, good to see you." Mike Woodson motioned them to sit, and passed out a handful of folders.

Jake took a seat next to Woodson and scanned the room. Seated around a long, shiny, black table were six people with stone-cold expressions. Jake didn't recognize a single one.

Woodson stood. "Alright let's get started." He clicked a few keys on his computer and the projector lit with a surveillance image Jake had taken from the compound.

"We've gathered here to organize an official task force for the Three Stooges," he glanced at Jake, "you can thank Thomas for that nickname." He turned back toward the projector. "Let's go over what we know."

"Exactly one week ago, a bomb threat was called in to the Arkansas State Capitol building. Although nothing transpired, it's important to note that the caller stated that this was *the beginning*. Of what? That's what we need to find out. Since that day, there have been two murders in Berry Springs, Arkansas, in roughly the same area where the Stooges' compound is located. The bodies either are, or loosely tied to, law enforcement and were branded with this symbol." He pointed to the screen. "Are the bodies connected to the Stooges? We don't know, yet, but that's exactly why we're here."

"Okay, so that's the highlights, now let's backup a minute." Three grainy, black-and-white pictures popped up side by side. "These are the three Stooges. From left to right—Scott Anderson; he appears to be the ring leader, Thad Deathridge, and Kyle Howard. We began tracking them six months ago when our scanners picked up continuous anti-government rants on their social media accounts. From there, we linked Scott's IP address to a website dedicated to banding anti-government 'renegades' together. However, the most interesting thing we found was that all three boys commonly visit a popular hunting blog and each are active bloggers. Their blog traffic picked up significantly in the days before the bomb threat. Here's the tough part, they talk in codes. Computer forensics expert Ethan Veech, is proactively working to decode, trace and track the trio." Veech nodded, Woodson continued.

"A week ago, an opportunity presented itself when I learned that Trainee Thomas was going to be in Berry Springs, Arkansas, for personal business. I assigned Jake to conduct surveillance on the compound, working under-cover. Since then, as I stated earlier, two dead bodies have piled up."

"Special Agent Woodson," a man with dark eyes and sharp features, named Conroy, raised his hand, "Do we have any evidence whatsoever that the bodies are connected to the Stooges?"

"No."

Conroy pressed his eyebrows together. "Then are we only working on suspicion?"

Woodson sat and turned to Veech. "Veech?"

Veech cleared his throat, "Maybe not just suspicion. I've been tracing the symbol branded on the bodies. As you can see on the screen, the symbol is a circle, with unidenti-fiable straight lines, angles and curves—we'll call them let-ters for now—inside the circle. I've spent hours unscram-bling the lines to make them readable." The room was dead silent. "After coming up with about three hundred possible combinations, I scanned each one." He nodded at Wood-son to click to the next slide. "This is the combination, or complete symbol, that I believe is tied to the Stooges."

Blank expressions stared at the screen, as Veech continued. "As you can see, an A, S, and B, are now identifiable in the circle."

Glancing at everyone's confused faces, Woodson leaned forward. "And, this is where we bring in our expert profiler, Mrs. Annette Angelini."

At the end of the table, a short woman in a long, brown skirt and flowing, pink, silk shirt stepped forward. Around her neck, hung at least ten necklaces, mainly turquoise stones.

"Thanks, Agent Woodson. To pick up where Veech left off—the initials A, S, and B, could possibly stand for Anglo Sons Brotherhood."

"Whoa, I thought these guys were anti-government, not white supremacists."

She smiled, "We don't believe they are white supremacists. Hang on, let me finish. Okay, so as most of you know, my job is to understand the suspects mind—the way they think, process and filter information. To begin to understand this, we need to dive into their childhoods."

She slid a stack of papers to the center of the table. "Inside you'll find the detailed reports that you can read later, and for time's sake, I'll hit the highlights." The photo on the projector switched to three older men. "These three men are the boys' fathers." She shook her head. "We've definitely got some winners here. All three of their fathers were involved in a white supremacy group called the ASB, in the 1970s and early '80s. Which as I already stated, is short for Anglo Sons Brotherhood. These were some evil dudes. Among many other charges, one was convicted of first-degree murder; the other two were in and out of jail their whole lives. All three have charges, or at least allegations, regarding child abuse. Each man is deceased now." She motioned to the report, "details are inside."

"Nice role models."

"Exactly. And as you can see in the picture behind me, each of their fathers ran in the same groups, were buddies. Their boys, our three Stooges, grew up together. The kids feel bonded through their fathers' friendships. There's no telling what each of these boys were subjected to at early ages."

"Do they have records?"

"Only our main guy, Scott Anderson. He went to juvie at age twelve for assault. He apparently beat a fellow dodgeball player within an inch of his life. The other two boys are clean. Now, here's where things start to get interesting. A cop popped Scott's dad twelve-years ago. It affected Scott deeply, and he blames the injustice of law enforcement."

The team was now fully engaged. Conroy raised his eyebrows. "Ah, things are starting to come together now. So, these kids had abusive childhoods and have bonded through that, and now they've grown up and refocused their anger through a common disdain for law enforcement."

She nodded. "Government in general, based on the Internet communications that Veech has provided. It's important to note that the boys might also have a disrespect for law enforcement because the system did nothing to protect them from their abusive families as children. That's how they see it."

"Why are they using their fathers' symbol as their own symbol now?"

"That's their common bond, their fathers."

"Why the branding?"

"Branding is almost always used by someone with an inflated ego. Someone who doesn't believe they can be caught, or in rare cases, doesn't care if they're caught. These boys are young and feel invincible. They laugh at law enforcement. But, I also think that in Scott's case, he wants to put fear into the town. He gets off on it." She motioned to the report on the table.

"My assessment of the men is detailed in the report. The net of it is this—Scott Anderson, now age twenty four, is very dangerous and since his father was *murdered* by law enforcement—that's how he sees it—he has now funneled his rage into revenge. Revenge for his father. Scott is, no doubt, the ringleader in this crew. You'll see in the report, the other two boys are also both in their mid-twenties. These two fall in line behind Scott and are more than happy to take orders from him."

She continued. "It's the typical story of someone who is lost, being taken in by someone perceived as a leader and then molded and used to the leader's liking. Think Hitler. Hell, think any terrorist group. Over half of terrorist group members are men in their upper teens and twenties who only desire to be a part of something. They are lost, and they are found. Just not by the right people. That's what you find in Thad and Kyle. And, don't get me wrong, these two are as dangerous as Scott, because they constantly feel that they have something to prove. They need to prove they are worthy. So, my headline is: These three men are evil dudes."

Jake leaned forward. "During my surveillance a few days ago, a woman visited the compound. Do we have her identity yet?"

A smile spread across Veech's face. "Yep, just last night."

Jake cocked his head, "Who is she?"

Still grinning, Veech leaned forward, clicked a few keys on the keyboard.

Jake raised his eyebrows and a few *whoot, whoots* erupted from the men in the room as the picture popped up on the monitor. In the center of a grainy black-and-white surveillance photo was a stunningly beautiful dark-haired woman with a body that would hypnotize most men. She wore tiny straps, which he assumed she considered to be a bathing suit.

Who is she?"

"Jolene Reeves, born and raised in Texas. At age fifteen, her mom, also from Texas, dragged Jolene with her to Chicago to be with one of her many lovers. I don't think she knows her real dad. Not a great childhood. Jolene moved back to Texas, alone, when she turned eighteen."

Still gazing at the photo, Woodson said, "She's been on our radar for about six months."

"She has? For what?"

"She's suspected to be involved in a small cyber-theft ring, part of a larger underground money laundering operation."

"Why hasn't she been brought in?"

"Can't pin anything on her and she's not the big fish we want, she's just a middleman, so to speak. We're trying to learn who she works for, or what group."

"What does she do?"

Veech glanced at the screen. "Well, she covers her tracks well. She's smart. But we believe she's responsible for getting smurfers, or mules, to illegally transfer stolen funds."

"Ah, so she uses her *assets* to lure unsuspecting marks in. She cons some idiot into transferring money for her, saying they get a small percentage?"

"Exactly. And she gets a bigger percentage of every transaction."

Woodson switched the screen to the photo of the blue barrels. "Which leads us here. This woman arrived the same day as these blue barrels. Presumed to be liquid. What liquid, we don't know and need to find out. But, boys... and Annette, this does not make me feel warm and fuzzy inside."

The team fell silent, letting the information sink in.

Conroy rubbed his chin, "Local law enforcement? How are they involved?"

Woodson tapped his pen on the table. "They're not, exactly. They are unaware of our surveillance of the Stooges, and as far as I can tell, the local police isn't even keeping their eye on them. They're preoccupied with the two recent murders, and are in a frenzy that both bodies are loosely linked to them. Which is a good segue way to our next topic. The two murder victims." He motioned to a younger man in a brown suit and tie. "This is Agent Fine."

"Thanks, Woodson." Agent Fine slid a stack of papers down the table, and then turned to the projector. "This is Amy Duncan, a local news reporter. Age twenty-seven, single, no kids. The full autopsy has not been completed yet, but thanks to Thomas who found the body, we know that she was gutted and branded with the symbol Woodson showed earlier."

"How does she tie to law enforcement?"

"She was having an affair with an Officer Carl Winters. Worst kept secret, the whole town knew about it."

"So, assuming one of the three Stooges killed her, they might have done it to shine a light on the immorality of law enforcement?"

"Exactly."

"Why aren't we assuming it was Officer Winters himself?"

"Good question, he is a suspect but nothing solid so far. And, the branding indicates the Stooges." Moving on, he clicked screens. "The body found last night is Officer Matt Danson. Best buds with the chief of police. Age thirty-six, married, one child. Been on the force for seven years. The autopsy is not complete, but it appears he was beaten, gutted, shot and branded. His badge was also pinned to his skin."

"Why do they have a beef with this guy?"

"Undetermined at this time, but could just be that he's a cop. Simple as that."

Woodson stood. "Thanks, Fine." He turned to the team. "I had an... interesting conversation with a Lieutenant Rubin from the Berry Springs force last night, and with Police Chief David McCord this morning." He cut Jake a glance, laced with warning. "We will work closely *with* them on a potential serial killer in the area. On exactly that. They now know that Jake is working with the FBI, but they don't know we are surveilling the Stooges yet. Not until we can officially tie them to the bodies. At that point, we will take over the case completely and Jake will remain in Berry Springs on the mission for the time being. Is that understood Trainee Thomas?"

Agent Conroy spoke up. "Jake Thomas is fresh out of training, and only a temp at this point. You're going to make him lead on this?"

Woodson narrowed his eyes, "Special Agent Conroy, you will accompany Jake back to Arkansas. You two will work as a team, is that understood?"

The vein in Conroy's neck pulsed as he glanced at Jake, then back at Woodson. "Yes, sir."

Woodson motioned to the packets that he had passed out at the start of the meeting. "Inside you'll find your individual assignments. Team, your goals here are to understand what threat the Stooges are, and to eliminate that threat. If the Stooges are not linked to the dead bodies, we will regroup and switch angles. Dismissed."

Ignoring the icy stare from Conroy, Jake pushed out of his chair.

From across the room, Woodson said, "Thomas, please stay behind."

Veech raised his eyebrows and elbowed Jake before leaving the room. Jake sat back down and turned toward Woodson. "Yes, sir?"

"I decided not to tell the team about your little stint in jail last night."

"Thank you, sir."

"Jake, you understand that you work *under* Agent Conroy in Arkansas, correct? He's going to run the show now. At this point, I find myself questioning your judgment, and mine for fighting for you to be part of us, for that matter."

"Yes, sir."

"You've already ruffled feathers within the community,

which is one of the main things you are taught to avoid while being undercover. You're supposed to be unnoticeable and forgettable to the community." He clenched his jaw. "I've pulled a few of my undercover men out of jail, but never an agent fresh out of training."

"Yes, sir."

"You're pushing it. Already."

Jake looked down.

"I've been able to keep this from the Director for now, but this is grounds for failing our program. Are you taking this seriously, Jake?"

His head snapped up. "Yes, sir."

Woodson took a deep breath and leaned back. "I recruited you from the Army because we need agents like you. We need men like you. You are the number one sharpshooter in the country, not to mention in the top fifteen percent on intelligence testing." He leaned forward, "Do you understand what an asset that is?"

Jake squared his shoulders. "Yes, sir." That was an honest response.

"Good. And do you understand what it takes to be an undercover agent? How physically and emotionally difficult it can be? Not to mention lonely? They don't have families, Jake. And if they do, they miss everything. Everything."

"I understand the sacrifice."

"Your mother still doesn't know about your involvement with us, correct?"

"Correct."

"Alright, then." He began to gather his folders. "You'll be in meetings all day, then will fly back to Arkansas with Conroy tonight."

"Yes, sir."

Woodson nodded, stood and made his way to the door.

"Agent Woodson?" Jake stood as Woodson turned around. "I'm ready and I'm committed. I'm ready for all of this, and I appreciate your willingness to take a chance on me."

"Good. Now get your ass to your next meeting." Woodson walked out the door.

CHAPTER 17

SHE WAS ALONE, walking through the woods at dusk. She was happy, content. The white lace dress she wore tickled her legs as it blew in the breeze. Her long hair lay braided down her back.

The squirrels and birds greeted her as she journeyed farther and farther off the trail.

Without warning, night fell and she realized that she was lost. All the animals were suddenly gone, the cool breeze halted and the woods were deathly silent.

Where was she? Her heart pounded as she turned in a circle, trying to decide what to do, where to go. Surely she'd been here before?

Suddenly, she was grabbed by her ankle and pulled to the ground. She screamed in horror, her dress ripped from her body as she was pulled across the dirt. Fighting, pulling at shrubs and blades of grass, she tried to get away but was dragged further and further into the darkness.

Finally, she was released. She scrambled to her feet and looked around, only to find two eyes glowing in the darkness.

"Help me." The eyes begged, in a low, soft voice. Her sister's voice. "Help me."

She stood frozen.

"Help me. You're close, Katie. Keep looking."

The eyes disappeared into the darkness, and she stood, silent. She stared into the darkness, her heartbeat hammering in her chest.

Whoosh!

The mangled corpse of her sister flew through the air and disintegrated into the darkness.

Katie jerked awake from her nap, her clothes soaked in sweat. Heart racing, she looked around the room and took a deep breath.

"It was just a dream." She took another deep inhale. "Thank God, it was just a dream." She sat up in bed and noticed night had fallen. How long had she been asleep?

After arriving home from the police station the night before, Katie found herself unable to sleep. She couldn't get the images of the bodies out of her head. But, more than that, she couldn't get McCord and the missing button off her mind.

Was he there the day Jenna died? Maybe the timing of the email was coincidence? Hell, was she just totally overreacting?

No matter how much she tried to convince herself that it was just a coincidence, she couldn't shake the unease and curiosity away.

She'd busied herself the following day by packing and driving multiple loads to the thrift store, and now, even after her cat nap, she was still officially exhausted.

She pushed off the mattress and padded to the kitchen

for some water. Eleven o'clock at night. She'd slept for five hours straight.

Gulping ice-cold water, she tried to shake the creepiness from the dream.

She needed to get the hell out of this house, this town. It was all too much.

She slowly sipped her water and suddenly felt the presence of… something.

The hair on the back of her neck stood up.

She lightly set down the glass, tiptoed to the edge of the kitchen and peered into the hall.

The front door was open. Barely open.

Her stomach dropped. She had locked the door, right?

She looked around for any kind of weapon and spotted a can of wasp spray on the counter. She'd read in a magazine that it was the next best thing to a gun. She guessed she was about to find out.

All senses on alert, she quietly crept down the hall and pulled the front door closed, locking it back. The click of the lock echoed off the walls.

She swallowed a scream as her cell phone rang.

"Hello?"

"Katie?"

She recognized the voice instantly. "Yes."

"It's Jake."

Lieutenant Rubin's warning to stay away from him flashed through her mind.

"Am I calling too late?"

"No." Her voice shook. "I'm awake."

He paused. "Are you okay?"

She hesitated as she gazed out the window. "Honestly, I don't know."

His voice switched from casual to clipped. "Katie, what's wrong?"

Should she tell him about the door being open? What good would that do? Why the hell was he calling her this late anyway? "Oh, never mind, everything's fine."

No response.

"Did you need something?"

He cleared his throat. "I just wanted to check on you."

She began walking around the house, checking each room to ensure she was alone. Better to be attacked while she's on the phone than completely alone.

"Thank you, I'm okay."

"Okay…"

She didn't know what to say. Why did this guy tongue-tie her so much? Instead of drawing out the awkward pause another second, she choked and said, "I need to go."

No response.

"Bye, Jake."

Click.

Katie lowered the phone and released an exhale. Shaking her head, she walked to the kitchen and poured a glass of wine.

Jake was calling to check on her. To make sure she was okay. Well, she was *not* okay.

She sipped her wine and stared blankly at the wall.

Not ten minutes later she heard a truck rumbling in the distance. Her pulse picked up as the sound got closer and closer.

She peered down the hall, out the window. Two headlights cut through the dark night, heading straight up her driveway.

Gripping the wine glass in one hand, she grabbed the can of wasp spray with the other and darted down the hall, hiding behind the den wall.

The engine cut off.

The truck door squeaked open, and then slammed shut.

She heard heavy footsteps through the gravel, up the porch steps, and then stop at the front door.

She held her breath.

Knock, knock, knock.

Her heartbeat spiked as she fumbled with the spray nozzle.

Knock, knock.

The doorknob turned, but it was locked. A few clicks later, the door creaked open and the intruder stepped inside.

Here we go.

She clenched her jaw and jumped from behind the wall. "Stop! Get out!" She pointed the spray at the intruder's face as wine sloshed all over the floor.

"Whoa!" Laughing, Jake raised his hands to surrender.

Her mouth dropped open. "Jake! You scared the hell out of me!"

Grinning, he looked at the spray. "Good thing I'm not a wasp, I'd be in big trouble."

She glared at him and lowered the can. "What are you doing here?"

"I came to check on you." He shifted his weight. "You didn't sound okay on the phone."

She didn't know if she was pissed or relieved, so she just stepped aside and motioned him inside.

He closed and locked the door, and looked around. "Nice place."

Eyeing him she said, "How the hell did you pick my lock?"

"Everyone knows how to pick a lock."

She glanced at the door with the sickening feeling that maybe he wasn't the only person to pick the lock this evening.

He shoved his hands in his pockets. "So, what's going on? What's got you so jumpy?"

"Nothing." She looked at him. At his massive, strong, sexy body. God, she felt out of control. Out of control, scared and so confused. And so damn attracted to him. They stood awkwardly in the hall until she remembered her manners. "Well, come on in. Would you like a drink?"

Something sparked in his eyes as he looked her up and down. The same spark she saw when he slid off of his horse, the first time they met.

Wearing a small smile, he nodded and followed her into the kitchen. As she poured him a drink, he watched her every move.

"You okay?"

Without responding, she handed him his glass.

He took a sip. "I'm not going to ask again."

Irked by his tone, she snapped back. "Two dead bodies are what's going on, Jake. Isn't that enough to be a little high strung?" Frazzled, she took a sip of wine and looked out the window. Her voice lowered. "And, I think someone might have broken in here tonight."

His back straightened, he set down his wine. "Here? While you were here?"

"Yes. No." She shook her head, "I don't know. I fell asleep and when I woke up, I noticed the door was unlatched."

He glanced down the hall. "Did you see anyone?"

"No."

He turned and walked out of the kitchen.

"What are you doing?"

"Searching."

"I said I didn't see anyone. I already checked through the house."

He ignored her as he checked each room, top to bottom. She wanted to stop him, but the reality was that she was relieved. Relieved to have him here. Relieved to have someone here to make sure she was safe. But was she safe with him?

He walked back in the kitchen and glanced outside. "The house is clear. Did you hear anyone outside?"

She shook her head.

"Okay." His eyes continued to search the room. "Any idea why someone would want to break in?"

"I told you, I'm not sure if someone did. But, no, I can't think of any reason someone would break in." She hesitated, thinking of McCord. Did McCord somehow know that she hacked into her sister's email? Did he see that she noticed the button missing from his shirt? Did he break in?

Jake picked up his wine, sipped and eyed her over the rim with a look that made it clear that he knew she was leaving out details.

"I'm sorry, I need some air." She stepped past him,

pushed through the screen door and sat down on the porch steps.

He followed her outside.

The humidity of the warm evening coated her skin as she gazed up at the dark night sky. With her back turned to him, she asked, "Who bailed you out?"

"Out of what?"

She rolled her eyes. "Jail, Jake. Who the hell bailed you out of jail?"

"A buddy."

"Oh, a buddy, huh?"

"They had nothing on me, you know that."

She didn't respond.

He took the seat next to her. The evening breeze swept across them and she caught the scent of fresh soap on his skin.

"Did your sister live here?"

She looked down and took a deep breath. "Yes, she'd just moved in." She leaned back on her elbows, gazed at the sky. "Being back is difficult. More difficult than I thought it would be. You know, I miss her every day. It's so hard being back. It brings that day right back in front of me, as if it happened yesterday."

"You were with her that day, right?"

"Yes. Well, yes, but I left her for just a little while to look for arrowheads." She shook her head. "Arrowheads."

A minute of silence ticked by.

"It wasn't your fault." He put his strong hand on her back.

Tears filled her eyes and the truth was that she did feel like it was her fault. Deep down she did blame herself. She couldn't count how many times, over the last year she'd berated herself for leaving her sister that day. To go look for arrowheads, of all things. If she would have never left, her sister would still be alive.

Her stomach began to churn.

"You don't think it was an accident, do you?"

"No."

"Why?"

"I found something, that day. On the cliff."

"What?"

She pushed herself off the steps, walked inside and back out a minute later.

"A button." She opened her palm.

He picked it up and turned it over in his fingers. "A shirt button."

She nodded and sat back down on the step.

"You found it on the cliff?"

"Yes, close to the edge."

"Hmm. On the day your sister died?"

She nodded.

He peered closer at it. "Could be anyone's."

Expressionless and lost in her own thoughts, she stared at the small button.

"But you don't think it's just anyone's."

"No, I don't."

"Did you tell the police?"

"No."

"Why?"

"I don't know. Honestly, the days following her death were such a blur, I didn't think about it. But, since I've been back, I've thought about bringing it up now."

"Don't."

"Why?"

"Just... let me handle it."

She cocked her head and looked him up and down. "Who the hell are you, Jake Thomas? I know someone with authority demanded your immediate release from jail. I know you can handle a gun. I know you aren't in the Army. So, who are you?"

He stared into the darkness for a moment before turning and looking at her. His hard expression softened as he gazed into her eyes.

Her breath caught. His mysterious, blue eyes twinkled in the moonlight, full of fire and an intensity that made her feel like she was completely under his control. Small, yet safe. As he looked at her, his muscular chest began to rise and fall in a steady rhythm. Butterflies danced in her stomach.

He slowly slid his hand onto her leg and tingles rippled through her body. His lips parted, she licked hers, and he leaned forward... and kissed her. Passionately kissed her. Melted her.

Her body went limp as he slid his warm tongue into her mouth. His lips soft, yet commanding, against hers.

Head spinning, her wineglass fell from her hand, shattering down the steps as she wrapped her hands around his body.

He pulled back and looked into her eyes. For a moment, his world stopped. His body vibrated with nerves, the same way it did when something big was about to happen. Something life-changing. For a moment, he hesitated. The non-committal, lone wolf inside of him hesitated.

Looking back at him, she blinked, her eyelashes sweeping against her brown eyes. Her expression filled with anticipation... and lust. And as she licked her lips, his hesitation melted away and was instantly replaced by an extreme need to have her. She had a power over him, something otherworldly that he simply couldn't resist.

She asked him who he really was. Should he tell her?

His heart started to pound as he reached up and slowly ran his fingers through her long hair. He leaned into her ear and whispered, "You're safe with me. I'm going to keep you safe, Katie."

Tears welled in her eyes and she crushed her lips on his.

He kissed her back, hard, and then softly lowered her onto the hardwood porch.

His large hand cradled the back of her head, his fingers tangled in her hair, as his lips slid over hers.

Her heart hammered as she pulled off his shirt. She gaped at his body—the perfectly chiseled chest, broad shoulders and six pack abs. He was simply perfect. She ran her fingers down his stomach and a slight smile crossed his lips before he leaned back over her.

He kissed her ear, her neck, and her chest, before sliding her shirt over her head. His hand found her bare breast and her skin prickled as he rubbed his finger around her nipples.

He leaned down, took her breast in his mouth and slowly removed her shorts. Adrenaline surged through her body as he tossed them across the deck. A warm breeze swept past her bare skin. She felt free. Desired. Hot.

And she had to have him right that second.

Right now.

She yanked off his pants, grabbed his shoulders and guided him onto his back. Her heart raced in anticipation for what was about to come. It had been so long since she'd felt the warm touch of a man.

She straddled him on her knees, leaned down and kissed him, her nipples rubbing against his sweaty chest. Her finger guided itself down his rock hard stomach, bumping over his six-pack. His grip on her waist tightened as her hand crept lower.

And, lower.

She felt his skin run with goosebumps as her finger danced around the base of his hard cock. He bit his lip, his eyes narrowed with a fire and intensity she'd never seen before. His chest began to rise and fall faster and faster. Finally, her fingers enclosed around his hardness.

He groaned and closed his eyes.

She lightly stroked, up, down, up, down, then squeezed. Harder. She knew he was already about explode.

Not yet.

He gripped her bare waist and flipped her onto her back.

She took a moment to look at him. Every inch of him. Every long, wide, hard inch of him.

Eyes wild with lust, he kneed her legs apart and lowered his head to her stomach, lightly kissing her belly button before lowering himself farther down.

Her body flushed with wetness as his tongue slid down her abdomen, to her lips. He lingered, teasing her before lightly circling around her clitoris. The heat began to rise between her legs as he licked harder and faster.

She pulsated with desire.

Just as she was about to lose all control, he raised up, looked in her eyes and lowered down on top of her.

His voice gravely, he whispered into her ear, "Get ready."

A surge of electricity shot through her body as he pushed himself inside of her.

"*Oh, Jake.*" Breathless, she dug her fingernails into his back.

He slowly slid out of her wetness, then plunged deeply back inside her.

Her breath caught.

With his soft lips on hers, he slid in and out. Deeper. Wetter.

With every thrust he rubbed her deep inside, her whole body responding to the pleasure.

She felt as if she couldn't breathe, as if she forgot how.

Their bodies dripped in sweat as they moved together, faster and faster.

Her clitoris began to tingle, flush with heat, with every thrust.

The sensation finally peaked, and as she arched her back, euphoria gripped her and she released. Her wetness flowed over him, her body squeezed around him.

"Katie…" Breathless, he said her name as he climaxed at the same time, filling her with everything he had in him.

For a moment, it was as if they were weightless, suspended in air, in the beautiful darkness.

He collapsed on top of her.

After a deep breath, he rolled onto his back and reached over and touched her hand.

Her body still tingling, her heart still racing, she closed her eyes and took a deep breath. The aftermath of the euphoria left her body as weak as jello, and as satisfied as she had ever been.

Eventually, he turned to her. A small, tired smile crossed his lips.

Her heart swelled.

Looking into her eyes, he swept a sweat-soaked strand of hair out of her face. "You're beautiful."

She smiled and whispered, "Thank you."

She pushed herself up on her elbows and looked past him, into the kitchen. "I'm hungry."

His boisterous laugh caught her off guard as he stood up, stark naked like a newborn baby. "I can cook."

"You can?" She grabbed his hand as he helped her up.

"Yep."

He followed her into the kitchen.

"I don't have much." She opened the fridge and the cold air coated her sweat in the best possible way. Thanks to a quick stop at the grocery store earlier, she had a few things, but nothing worth writing home about. "This might be the test of a lifetime for a cook."

He walked up, wrapped his arms around her and lightly kissed her forehead. "I'll make do."

She smiled up at him. "Okay then. I'll go get dressed."

As he went to work in the kitchen, she walked across the house to her bathroom and glanced in the mirror. She was positively glowing. Relaxed. Happy.

She splashed some water on her face, smoothed her matted hair and slipped into a cotton night dress. She took one last glance in the mirror and decided to apply a little lip-gloss before making her way back to the kitchen.

The smell of bacon floated through the air, sending her

stomach growling. She walked into the kitchen to find him cooking in his boxer shorts.

"Smells good."

He glanced over his shoulder, "Cute dress. I make the best scrambled eggs this side of the Mason Dixon."

She popped two slices of bread in the toaster and leaned against the counter, taking in every inch of him. He looked like a Greek God statue. She'd only seen bodies like that in the movies. And, my God, she just had sex with him.

Her cheeks flushed as the toast popped up.

"Perfect timing." He scooped the eggs on two plates, added a couple pieces of bacon and walked to the kitchen table. Katie grabbed the toast, butter and... wine. Yes, more wine.

They sat across from each other and she watched him scoop a forkful of eggs into his mouth.

They had just had the best sex of her life and now here they were, sitting across from each other at the kitchen table, eating a prepared meal and drinking wine. Their relationship—if you want to call it that—had gone from dead bodies to extremely intimate in less than an hour.

She bit into her toast as Jake asked, "Where exactly was the button?"

"The edge of the cliff."

"How close?" He shoveled more eggs into his mouth.

"Close. A few feet."

"Did you notice anything else?"

"No."

"Nothing? Footprints? Blood?"

"No. But... her scream. She screamed twice."

"Twice?"

She nodded. "I thought it was strange too. One scream makes sense. But two screams... two screams makes me think there was something else. Maybe a struggle of sorts."

"You told the police that you heard two screams?"

"Yes."

Jake thought about that for a moment. "Who completed the autopsy?"

"I actually don't know."

He nodded and scooped the last bit of eggs into his mouth. "Do you have a plastic bag?"

"In the drawer, over there."

He picked up the button from the table, walked to the counter and placed it in a plastic bag. "Don't lose this."

She nodded.

After cleaning up dinner, she curled up next to him on the porch swing and listened to the sounds of the warm summer night. Clouds drifted across a dark sky, occasionally blocking the bright moon. A light breeze cooled the temperatures enough to make it almost tolerable.

She nestled in his arms, and not surprisingly, fell fast asleep.

⋐

Jake noticed her heavy inhales and exhales, and realized she had fallen asleep cradled in his arms. After stroking her soft, silky hair a few more times, he carefully carried her to her bed.

He hesitated.

It was a perfect opportunity to sneak out, which was what he was accustomed to. His hesitation caught him off guard—which was something he was not accustomed to. Not much caught him off guard.

He looked down at her. A break in the clouds let the glow of the moon seep in through the window, illuminating her face with an angelic silver light. Her beautiful face.

He watched her. Watched her sleep, the shallow rise and fall of her chest. She slept happy, almost with a small smile on her face.

He smiled and something inside him stirred. Something deep inside of him. He reached over and brushed a strand of hair out of her face. She was stunning, but she was so much more than that. He wanted to know everything about her. He wanted to see that same spark in her eyes that he saw while they were making love—every single day.

But, most of all, he wanted to make sure she was safe. And something in his gut told him she wasn't.

Before he could talk himself out of it, he slid into bed next to her, rolled on his side and watched her until he finally fell asleep.

The next morning, Jake rose before the sun.

He silently pushed out of bed and tiptoed down the hall, into the kitchen. He plucked his keys off the counter and turned to leave.

But halfway down the hall, he paused.

He turned and eyed the plastic bag with the button sitting on the kitchen table. After listening a moment to make sure she was still asleep, he grabbed it off the table and with the bag tucked safely in his pocket, jumped in his truck and rolled in neutral silently down her driveway.

CHAPTER 18

"CONROY." JAKE SLID into the booth across from his temporary, *and temperamental*, supervisor.

Agent Conroy looked up from his menu and gave a swift nod. "Jake."

It didn't go unnoticed by Jake that Conroy called him by his first name when everyone in the Agency was addressed by their last name. It was undoubtedly an attempt to undercut him and remind him who was boss.

"Morning, gentlemen." A smooth smile slid across Diner Debbie's red lips. Her cleavage spilled from her blouse, which was halfway unbuttoned.

Both Conroy and Jake took a moment to soak in the view before responding. "Morning."

"Can I get ya'll some coffee?"

They both nodded.

She smiled. "Ya'll aren't from here, are you?"

"No."

"What brings you to little Berry Springs? You stick out like sore thumbs." She winked.

"We're contractors, here on business."

"Ah, yes, you look like businessmen." After glancing at Jake's bare ring finger, she said, "I'll give you boys a moment to look over the menu and I'll be back with coffee."

Conroy raised an eyebrow as she walked away. "Something about Southern women."

Jake hid his smile. He'd just had an unforgettable evening with a certain Southern woman, and, yeah, there sure as hell was something about her.

Conroy reached into his folder and slid a piece of paper across the table. "We've got developments."

Jake scanned the highlighted conversations between the Stooges.

"Their communications are picking up, heavily."

"Since when?"

"Just last night. Looks like they're getting ready for something."

Jake nodded. "They've got times and dates here, but they're in the past."

"Right, but it certainly means something. It's a code."

"Veech on it?"

Diner Debbie sauntered up and delicately placed two cups on the table, bending over a little more than she needed to. Her breasts were on full display as she poured the steaming coffee and looked at Jake. "So, have you decided what you'd like to eat this morning?" She winked.

Jake ignored the innuendo. "Pancakes, double stack."

She raised her eyebrows, "Double stack? Impressive."

She turned to Conroy who was doing his best to hide his grin. "I'll take the same."

"Two double stacks. I'll be back."

After watching her dance away, Conroy lowered his voice. "I think she'd like a bite of your double stack."

"I'm sure she's had more than a few double stacks."

Conroy almost laughed. *Almost*. But then got down to business. "Anyway, yes, Veech is working to decode it as we speak. Until then, I'd like to survey the compound."

"I planned on doing that right after we met here."

"Fantastic. We'll go together."

Jake clenched his jaw. He preferred to survey alone and certainly didn't need some uptight suit blowing his cover.

Reading his expression, Conroy leaned forward. "You're on a tight leash, Jake. A leash that you created for yourself."

Jake narrowed his eyes. "Do you have a problem with me, Agent Conroy?"

"You bet your ass I do. For reasons I don't understand, you were recruited to be part of an elite group of men and women. And what have you done with that? On your first week out of training? You got yourself thrown in jail, creating unnecessary tension between us and local law enforcement. And you were only supposed to be conducting surveillance for Christ's sake," he sipped his coffee, "being an undercover agent isn't just running into burning buildings, guns blazing and saving the world, Jake. It takes patience, restraint and an intense personal awareness above all. You have to be likeable, trusted, and be able to adapt to any and all situations. Unlike what you've done here."

Jake felt his fists clenching under the table just as Debbie slid his double stack across the table.

He picked up his fork and cut into his pancakes. Restraint. It didn't come easy to him. But, through years in the Army, he learned the skill the hard way and he decided to practice it now, and keep his mouth shut. His mom always told him that silence was more powerful than yelling.

After finishing their breakfast, they stepped out into the parking lot.

"We'll take my truck."

Conroy nodded and after retrieving a bag from his rental car, he climbed into the passenger seat. His phone rang before Jake pulled out of the gravel parking lot and Conroy proceeded to take calls during the drive to the mountain, which didn't bother Jake much, considering he had no desire to make bullshit small talk with the suit.

After a few miles down a dirt road, the truck rolled to a stop at the bottom of the hill and Jake glanced over at Conroy. "You bring shoes? Hell of a climb for those loafers."

"I think I'll make it."

"Suit yourself." Jake jumped out of the cab, pulled his backpack out of the back and changed into hiking boots. He grabbed his scope and gun and stepped through the brush as Conroy followed.

The sun beat down on them as they maneuvered through the trail. The humidity had doubled since breakfast. By the time they reached the top of the mountain, they were drenched in sweat.

Jake set up his gear and got into position as Conroy peered through his binoculars.

"Are those the blue barrels you were talking about?"

"Yep, they've moved them."

"Same amount?"

"Yep."

Jake zoomed in on the front door of the main house

as Stooge number two, Kyle Howard stepped outside. "Got movement."

"That Kyle?"

"Yep, looks like he's got an overnight bag."

"Hmm."

Jake watched as Stooge Two loaded a bag into the trunk of a car, and then disappeared into the office. Moments later, he walked out carrying a taped up box and carefully placed it in the truck next to the duffle bag. After slamming the trunk closed, Kyle walked back into the main house and moments later, all three Stooges walked outside, to the car.

After a brief conversation, they shook hands and embraced in a hug.

Jake raised his eyebrows.

"Hug? I didn't take Scott as a hug kind of guy."

"Me either." Jake's gut churned. "Looks like a good luck and goodbye to me."

Conroy lowered his binoculars and looked at Jake. "I don't like that one bit. Get the license plate."

"Already did." Jake rattled off the number and Conroy scribbled in a small notebook, then grabbed his phone.

"No service up here."

"Dammit. We need to get him tailed."

"And inform security at the Capitol building to be on the lookout for that car."

Conroy nodded. "How far is the capitol building from Berry Springs?"

"Forty-five minutes, give or take."

Agitated, Conroy ran his fingers through his sweaty hair. "Veech needs to break the damn code. We either need to be here, or there. And we can't waste time driving if something happens."

"Can we get someone there?"

He shook his head. "We're stretched thin as is. Until we have something concrete, our hands are tied and Woodson isn't open to putting any more boots on the ground."

"We've got two dead bodies branded with the same symbol that link back to the boys' fathers."

"Right, but the symbol interpretation is technically a guess at this point."

Irritated at the red tape, Jake shook his head. "It's a damn good guess, and you know it. Come on, Conroy, it all fits."

Conroy's eyes leveled on him. "Let me reiterate for you, we don't know definitively if the bodies are connected to the Stooges. That's the bottom line. Until then…"

Jake looked away. Every inch of his gut told him that the two murders and the three men were connected.

"I'm going to head back down the mountain, make some calls. We had reception at your truck."

"I'm going to watch a bit longer."

"Sounds good."

∽

"McCord here."

"We found the car."

"Amy's?"

"Yep. Down County Road 29, by the river. About a mile on the other side of the water, from where her body was found."

"Right in front of our fucking eyes."

"Yes, sir. It's being photographed and searched now."

"Any signs of struggle?"

"No, car's in good shape."

"Blood?"

"Not that I can see. But, her cell phone and purse are not in the car."

McCord rubbed the stubble on his chin. "Thanks Jameson, let me know what they find."

"Yes, sir."

Just as he laid the receiver down, the phone rang again.

"What?"

"Chief, it's Jessica."

He blew out a breath. This would be about body number two, Officer Matt Danson. "Give it to me."

"The full autopsy isn't complete yet, but the cause of death is strangulation."

"What about the bullet holes?"

"He was shot post mortem."

He took a moment to let that news sink in. "So, the branding is the same, but his death is very different than Amy Duncan's."

"Yes, and yes, the branding is the exact same symbol."

His jaw clenched. No doubt that both murders are connected and it won't be long until the media alludes to a *serial killer*. On one hand, the branding news is good news because it makes Officer Carl Winters less likely of a suspect in his mistress's death. On the other hand a... serial killer.

"And the symbol is definitely burned into the skin?"

"Yes, like with a cattle prod."

He tapped his desk. "A customized cattle prod..." Shit,

how many of those are there in the south? "Okay, send me the full report once you're done."

"Yes, sir."

He hung up and glanced at the clock. "Dammit." He pushed himself out of his chair, grabbed a folder off of his desk and walked up front.

"Hey." Carl wiped his sweaty palms on his jeans as he stood up.

"Hey, Carl." McCord stepped aside and motioned Officer Carl Winters past the locked doors.

"Your office?"

McCord shook his head. Unfortunately, this was an official meeting. "Interview room two."

Carl shook his head, shoved his hands into his pockets and followed McCord down the hall.

Heads shot up from the bullpen. It was as if all the air was sucked out of the room. Calls stopped, chitchat stopped. The station was silent as they walked into the interview room.

All eyes were on Officer Winters. Did he kill Amy Duncan, his mistress? If so, did he kill Officer Danson too? Why?

McCord motioned him to sit as he pulled out a metal chair, its legs squeaking loudly across the floor.

He leaned forward. "Look, before I turn on the recorder… you know how this is going to go, I'll ask you about your whereabouts on the day of Amy's death, and ask you to confirm your alibis, etcetera."

Carl's face was white as a sheet.

McCord ran his hand over his bald head. "You know last night's murder was Danson, right?

Carl nodded. Although he was on official leave, nothing was a secret in this town.

"Carl, did you kill Amy?"

"Of course not."

"Did you kill Danson?"

"Fuck you, McCord."

McCord nodded. "I had to ask." He took a deep breath, "I want you to know that I know you didn't do it. Couldn't have."

"What are you getting at, McCord?"

"There's details I can't share with you, but *confidentially*, you need to know these two murders are connected. So, stop shitting yourself."

"Connected? How?"

"I can't get into that."

Carl shook his head and placed his clenched fists on the table. "Who the fuck would do that to him? Danson was a good guy. A good, fucking guy. And Amy?" He looked down. "Amy."

"I'm trying to figure that out, but I've got to clear you first, specifically from Amy's murder, you understand?"

"The whole fucking town already thinks I did it. Do you understand *that*? Whether you clear me or not, the gossip will never go away."

McCord's face dropped as he looked at Carl. He was right. Carl would always be looked at as a cheating murderer, and he knew it. Carl was crumbling. Falling apart.

"You've got to keep it together. Let's get through this." Pause. "How's the wife?"

Inhaling deeply, Carl looked down and shrunk into his

chair. "Not good, man. She's not good. I think this is it. She's going to leave me."

"Shit, Carl I'm sorry." Guilt twisted in McCord's stomach. "Affairs happen all the time though… especially in this profession. Shit man, I'll bet eighty-percent of my men have had affairs. Won't she understand one slip up?"

"Not when the affair is connected to a damn *murder*, McCord."

A moment of silence ticked by.

"Well that's why I've got to clear you of this, now. I'll hold a press conference; get the media to back off." He leaned forward. "I'll get this cleared for you immediately, you have my word. But, I need you to help me out with something."

Carl pressed his eyebrows together. "If you clear me as soon as possible, I'll do whatever the hell you ask."

"Good. I… I can't ask this of anyone else right now. But, I need you to keep your eye on two people. Tail them. Keep your eyes and ears open."

"Who?"

"An FBI agent…"

"An agent? How the hell am I going to tail a FBI agent?"

"Yeah an agent. Just be careful, alert."

"What the hell is the FBI doing in town?"

"They said he's in town visiting his mom. But Carl, this son-of-a-bitch showed up and then there were two murders back-to-back, and as if that's not enough, he was the one who found the bodies."

"He found *both* bodies?"

"Yep."

"Pretty fucking convenient."

"Exactly. He rubs me the wrong way."

"Who else?"

"You remember Katie Somers?"

Carl searched his memory. "I think so… oh, she's Jenna's sister, or was, right?"

"Yeah. She's been hanging out with him. I want to know what the hell they're up to."

"Okay."

"She should be easy to follow. Keep this between us, okay?"

He nodded.

"Okay," McCord grabbed the recorder, "The sooner we get this interview done, the sooner I can clear your damn name."

He wrung his hands together. "Let's get this shit done."

CHAPTER 19

KATIE GLANCED IN the rearview mirror—for the hundredth time—as sweat slicked her palms, making the steering wheel loose in her grip. One by one, she wiped each hand on her shorts and tried to steady her breathing.

She looked in the rearview one more time. Was she being followed? She swore she saw the same sedan at the gas station too. Surely not. No way.

Her pulse picked up as she turned onto the road.

What the hell are you doing? You're going to get yourself killed tonight. She pushed the thought away. No matter how many times she'd almost turned around, she knew that she wouldn't be able to rest until the proof was right in front of her.

She turned off her headlights and slowly pulled into a driveway with a *For Sale* sign out front, a few houses down from Chief McCord's.

It's now, or never.

She pulled her baseball cap down low and took a deep

breath. Twirling her sister's ring around her finger, she thought, *this is for Jenna. I'm doing this for her.*

She slipped her phone, flashlight and credit card in her pocket.

One more deep breath and she slid out of the car and pulled on a pair of blue latex gloves. She quickly glanced around before cutting through the lawn to the back of the vacant house. She'd have to cross three backyards without being seen.

In a slow jog, she glanced up at the dark, moonless sky.

Her heart thrummed in her chest as she slipped through the back property lines as quiet as a mouse. Thank God, there were no dogs.

Almost there.

She paused at the back fence. His house was dark. Good. She'd already confirmed he was out for the evening, but better safe than sorry.

She hopped the fence, crouched down and scurried across the back lawn.

Wind chimes sang lazily in the breeze.

Looking over both shoulders, she stepped onto the back deck, tiptoed up to the door and pulled the credit card out of her pocket.

It was a hell of a gamble considering she didn't know if McCord had an alarm system or not. And honestly, she'd be surprised if he didn't. But that was a risk she was willing to take.

Gripping the doorknob with one hand, she slid the credit card in between the door frame and the lock.

She jiggled the knob. No luck.

Again. No luck.

AMANDA MCKINNEY

She set her jaw and slid it in one last time.

Pop!

The door pushed open.

No alarm. Luck was on her side tonight.

The faint smell of a Mexican microwave dinner filled her nose as she stepped inside and tiptoed through the kitchen.

The *tick, tick, tick* of the large grandfather clock in the living room broke the silence as she stepped down the hall.

Surprisingly, the house was thoughtfully decorated, with each room having a theme of sorts. Red paint, apple dish towels, and an apple clock set the theme for the kitchen. The living room had a masculine hunting theme. The bathroom, a beach scene. In the hall hung dozens of pictures. Family pictures. Ex-wives?

She padded further down the hall. Where the hell is the master bedroom? She passed the living room, staircase and office, and *bingo*! The bedroom.

It smelled of fresh perfume. Gardenia. He hadn't been alone this evening.

She walked to the closet, put the flashlight in her mouth and began rifling through his clothes. Minutes ticked by as she went through the dozens of shirts.

Where the hell was it?

Panic began to wash over her. She knew she needed to get the hell out of there, but she couldn't leave empty handed. She'd risked too much already. Frantically, she searched the top shelves. Nothing. Her sixth sense was gnawing at her, telling her she needed to leave. Exhaling, she stepped out of the closet and walked across the room.

She stopped in her tracks. The hamper. She briskly stepped over, bent down and began going through the dirty clothes.

Her heart skipped a beat when she saw it. The red plaid shirt with white pearl buttons—one missing. There it was.

Time to go.

She wadded it up and began to turn when, *Whoosh!*

Terror shot through her as her head snapped back. The flashlight dropped from her mouth and bounced on the hardwood floor.

"What the hell are you doing in my house?" His voice snarling, McCord gripped her pony tail tighter, pulled her neck back. Pain vibrated to the top of her head.

Something hard pressed into her side. A gun.

"I'll ask you one more time before I kill you, what the hell are you doing in my house?" His warm, wet breath moistened her neck.

"Please, Chief McCord." Her voice came out in a whisper. "Please, don't."

"Keep your arms up and get on your knees."

Her whole body shaking, she sank to her knees.

"Who are you?" He stood behind her and she knew without question that the gun was aimed at her head.

"Katie. Katie Somers."

"*Katie Somers*? What the *fuck*? Turn around!" He flicked on a light.

Remaining on her knees, she turned around. "McCord, I'm sorry…"

"What the *fuck* are you doing breaking into my house?"

She hesitated for a moment. Her voice shook. "I know, McCord."

"You know what?"

"About the email, between you and my sister, the day before her death."

A moment of silence slid between them. Finally, he lowered his gun and looked down.

"Did you have something to do with it?"

His eyes cut to hers. "Did I have something to do with what, exactly, Miss Somers? Your sister's death?"

She stared at him.

"Of course I didn't have anything to do with it!"

She stood and shook the shirt at him. "The button. I found the button, McCord. At the scene."

"What button?"

"The button that's missing from this shirt."

He looked at the plaid shirt crumpled in her hand. Taking a moment to digest everything, he took a deep breath, set his gun on the dresser and pulled the shirt from her hands. "You found the button missing off *this* shirt, on the cliff, the day your sister died?"

She nodded.

He raised his index finger and motioned her to follow him. Katie watched him turn and step out of the bedroom. For a moment, she glanced at the window and considered jumping out and making a run for it.

No. She had to see this through.

She followed him down the hall and into the living room. He turned on a lamp, walked across the room to a small desk and opened the drawer.

"Sit."

He took a seat next to her on the couch and opened his palm. "You mean, this button?"

In his palm lay a white, pearl button that matched the others on the shirt. "This is the button from that shirt. I've been meaning to sew it on."

Katie blinked in disbelief.

McCord's eyes softened and he leaned forward. "Katie, I didn't kill your sister."

She was speechless and utterly humiliated.

He continued. "She and I were friends and she had come to me, confidentially, months before her divorce asking me to track Zach, and confirm that he was having an affair. So, I did, and sure enough, he was. She and I communicated through email to keep things quiet." He put his elbows on his knees and looked at the carpet. "I'll admit… I did have feelings for your sister, always had. Deep feelings. So, I helped her out, and tried to woo her in the process."

Katie swallowed the lump in her throat. "But the email said you were going to meet her the next day… the day she died."

He blew out an exhale. "I was going to take her horseback riding and to lunch. Like I said, I was pretty crazy about her, to be honest. She was… she was so full of life, and fun, and beautiful. But, she sent me a text in the morning saying she wouldn't be able to go, because you had come to town. And the next thing I know, I'm responding to a call about a body fallen from a cliff." His eyes saddened. "You weren't the only one devastated that day."

Katie shrunk with embarrassment. Eventually, she said, "So, you tailed Zach? You're the reason she knew he was cheating on her?"

He nodded. "She had her suspicions, but, yes, I caught him."

"Did Zach know he was being followed?"

"No, he had no clue."

She looked at McCord. "Maybe… he killed her?"

McCord looked up. "Why do you assume she was murdered?"

"She didn't fall. *She didn't*. We had been to that cliff a hundred times growing up. She didn't fall."

Aggravated, he pushed off the couch. "Well, I can tell you one thing for sure, that son-of-a-bitch Zach didn't do it. I verified every single one of his alibis. They're solid. You have to believe me when I tell you that I put that poor kid through the wringer. Trust me." He placed his hand on the fireplace mantle. "Between you and me, I wonder if she truly fell that day too, but I did everything I could do. There was nothing to raise suspicion and the case was closed."

"What if Zach paid someone else to do it?"

"No. I had Jonas hack into his email and phone records. Checked every email address and phone number personally. He didn't do it, Katie."

Maybe it was the adrenaline, the emotions, or something else, but rage bubbled up and Katie screamed, *"Someone did it, McCord."*

And with that exclamation, uncontrollable tears began to fall down her cheeks.

"Katie, calm down."

Shaking her head, she stood up. "I'm sorry for breaking in." She turned on her heel, ran down the hall and out the back door.

⤆

It took the drive home to calm down. She hadn't cried like that in years.

After a long, hot bath, she went out to the back porch to

gaze at the stars, wine in hand. She closed her eyes and laid her head back on the porch swing. What a night. She had literally committed a felony tonight—breaking and entering.

She took a deep breath.

She was going crazy. *Crazy*!

The swing swayed back and forth in the breeze and she thought of Jake. She hadn't heard from him since the day before. Since their incredible, explosive, mind-boggling sex. Goosebumps broke out on her arms just thinking about it.

He was a mystery to her. A rugged, handsome, mystery of a man that sure knew how to handle himself in the bedroom.

But, he was only in town temporarily. And so was she.

Jake would go back to whatever life he's living, wherever that is. And she would go back to work. Would they stay in touch? Would he think of her? Would she think of him?

There was something about the spark in his eyes when they made love. Something more than just lust. She knew it. Hell, she felt it over every inch of her body.

I'm going to keep you safe. No man had ever said that to her and she never thought she needed to hear it. But, coming from Jake, she realized she wanted to feel safe more than anything in the world. To be taken care of, physically and emotionally. To be safe in his arms. Safe in his huge, muscular arms.

With an inhale, she whispered to herself, "But, it's going to end, Katie. You're both leaving." And, suddenly, she felt a pang of anger.

Why the hell was he so secretive? And didn't she know

better than to get involved with someone like that? She'd probably never see him again.

He was a mistake. Coming back to Berry Springs was a mistake.

She thought about the last conversation she had with Bobby, about the dig in North Carolina that was just waiting for her to kick off. Usually, she'd be excited. Ecstatic. But, she wasn't. She felt like there had been a shift in her. Something changed, and she was never going to be the same again.

Here she was, back in her suffocating small town, reliving her sister's horrific death, and finding two dead bodies in the process. *And* making love to the most beautiful man she'd ever laid eyes on. *And* breaking into the police chief's house.

McCord was innocent. And while that relieved her, it also made her realize just how much she really thought that her sister's death was no accident.

Who would kill her sister?

Restless, she walked inside and into the den where Jenna's laptop sat on the floor.

She stared at it. She felt guilty going through it, but couldn't ignore the pull she felt to open it. So, she did. Again.

She sat on the floor and scrolled through her sister's email again. Nothing suspicious other than McCord's old emails.

"Hmm..." She opened the browser and clicked on history. Shopping sites, video sites, nothing unusual. Until,... Katie cocked her head... a dating site. *A dating site?* Jenna was on a dating site?

Why the hell was her sister on a dating site? Hell, she'd only been officially divorced a week.

Katie felt a surge of adrenaline as she clicked on the username and password. Thankfully, the username auto populated to: Jen0326. Katie's birthday.

She clicked on the password and bit her lip in deep thought. If this were like most secure sites, she'd be locked out after three tries.

What would Jenna's password be?

She tried their birthdays, combined.

Nope.

She took a sip of wine. *Come on Jenna, what would your password be?* Knowing that her sister wasn't the most cautious person in the world, she tried the obvious, "password."

Nope. Dammit. One more try.

She sat back and gazed out the window. Suddenly, it hit her.

She smiled as she typed her last guess. Greta. Their horse.

Bingo! The site opened up to Jenna's homepage. Katie smiled at the picture of her sister. She was so beautiful.

She scrolled down and a small blinking light caught her attention. Ten new messages from interested suitors, all after Jenna had died. She scrolled down to the last opened message.

The message was dated the day Jenna died.

Katie's heart started to pound as she opened the message from 08AS17B61.

Can't wait to meet you today. See you soon…

Katie's stomach dropped to her feet.

She looked at the time the message was sent—eight-thirty in the morning, right before their hike. She remembered how glued to her cell phone Jenna was that morning.

Did Jenna respond?

She scrolled to the sent messages. Empty.

She clicked back on the message and read it again.

"Okay, maybe this is a coincidence, Katie, calm down, this really doesn't mean anything."

She clicked on 08AS17B61's profile page, which was mostly blank. No picture, just age and general statistics like not married, no kids, etc.

Suddenly, a ding chimed from the computer.

08AS17B61 is online.

A chill ran up her spine.

She hovered the mouse over the name. Her palms began to sweat. She closed her eyes and clicked.

Two options popped up. Send message or wink?

Her hands trembled as she contemplated.

Send message.

A blank box popped up.

Slowly, she typed *Hello.*

Send.

Her heart pounded as she waited. A minute ticked by. *Ding.* 08AS17B61 is offline.

"*Dammit!*"

CHAPTER 20

KATIE'S ATTENTION WAS ripped away from the computer screen when she heard the low rumble of a truck coming up the driveway. She glanced at the clock, almost midnight.

She slid the laptop off of her knees and walked to the window.

As the truck came into view she remembered it instantly and butterflies awoke in her stomach. She took a moment to glance in the mirror and smooth her hair before walking to the door.

The truck rolled to a stop. After a minute, the door opened and six-foot-two inches of the sexiest man alive stepped out onto her driveway. She opened the front door and leaned against the frame.

"You know, cell phones work around here."

A smile curved on Jakes lips as he stepped onto the porch. "Nothin' like seeing the real thing."

She almost blushed. *Almost.* "It's late."

He paused, breaking his stride. "Too late?"

She looked him up and down. He wore a thin gray,

T-shirt, worn jeans and flip-flops. His stubble was freshly shaved and his dark hair a little tamer than usual. She stepped back and opened the door wider.

He stepped inside and looked down at her, their body's only inches apart. He smelled like fresh air.

"I just came by to check on you, again."

Her heart swelled and she smiled. "Two nights in a row, huh?"

"You'll get my bill."

The sexual tension began to mount. Already.

He stared into her eyes, assessing her. Then, he glanced around the house and his eyes landed on the glowing laptop. "What are you researching?"

Shit. "Oh, um, nothing."

He pushed passed her and walked into the den. Before she could grab it, he picked up the computer and raised his eyebrows and said, "You're on a dating site?"

Embarrassed, she snapped the laptop away. "No, no I'm not."

"Looks like you were on a dating site."

"No, I'm not on a dating site. Not that it's any of your business." Why the hell would he care anyway?

An awkward silence filled the room and she began to feel uncomfortable. Uncomfortable because of his reaction. Uncomfortable about how he made her feel embarrassed about being on the damn website. Uncomfortable because she felt vulnerable, and uncomfortable because this was the most relationship-like moment she'd had in years.

So, true to form, she went on defense.

"Look, about last night…" she took a deep breath,

"I'm leaving in a few days. Tomorrow, hopefully. And so are you… at least I think you are."

His jaw twitched as he listened to her. She could tell his mind was running a mile a minute but not a single word left his mouth.

"What do you do, Jake? What's your job?"

No response.

"Are you in the Army or not?"

"No. Not anymore."

"So, what do you do then?"

In a very firm, matter-of-fact tone, he responded, "I can't talk about it, Katie."

She threw her hands up and sarcastically said, "Oh well, okay, Mister CIA or FBI or whatever you are." Something sparked in his eyes and she began to pace. "For all I know, your avoidance to my questions means that you did kill the people in the woods. McCord sure seems to think so."

"You think I'm responsible for those murders?"

"You tell me. Hell, you show up and all the sudden two people are brutally murdered, what am I supposed to think?"

"Now you're sounding like McCord."

Her stomach clenched. And even though she didn't believe it, she said, "Well, maybe he's right."

"Are you done?"

Was she done? Didn't he know that was one of the many things you never say to a woman? "No, I'm not done. You say you're helping your mom move in. Bullshit. You won't tell me what you do for a living, or why you're truly here." She put her hands on her hips, "And on top of that, you and I... you and I... well, it was a *mistake*, okay?"

For a brief moment his eyes widened. Then, expressionless, he shoved his hands in his pockets and said, "Well, I'm glad to know how you feel about it."

She stopped pacing. *Dammit, don't do this Katie. Don't chase him away. Stop.*

He stood still for a moment, waiting for her to say something else. When she didn't, he stepped past her, toward the door.

In a quiet voice, she closed her eyes and said, "Jake..."

But it was too late.

She listened to the front door close. His heavy steps down the driveway. The roar of the engine, and the rumble of his truck as it faded into the night.

"*Dammit*, Katie." She wanted to punch something. She wanted to run. She wanted to get the hell out of there. Immediately.

Before she went bed, she made a promise to herself. She would get everything done that she needed to and be out of this godforsaken town by tomorrow night.

Tomorrow night.

∽

"Yo, Veech."

"Damn, dude, it's late."

"You never sleep."

"Got me there. Damn job. What you need?"

Jake's truck bumped over the dirt road, his headlights

cutting through the dark night. "I need you to look into something for me."

"Online or offline?"

"Offline."

"You got it, bro."

"Thanks." He cleared his throat. "I need you to identify two usernames on a dating site."

He pulled his phone away from his ear as Veech boisterously laughed. "You're on a dating site? Come on man, is Berry Springs really that bad?"

"It's not mine. Got a pen and paper?"

"Yep."

"Jen0326 and 08AS17B61."

"Alright, I will look into it. I'm buried though, you know."

"I know, priorities first, just get to it when you can."

"Will do."

"Any progress on the decoding the hunting blog?"

Veech exhaled loudly. "Why do you think I'm up so late?"

"Maybe a little shut-eye will help clear the head."

"You might be right. What the hell are you doing up so late?"

"Just checking on some things. I'm headed to do some night surveillance now."

"Conroy with you?"

"Nope." He was supposed to be.

Jake heard the chuckle through the phone. "Be careful, man."

"Will do. Get some sleep."

"See ya, bro."

"See ya."

⚜

Katie rolled over and opened her eyes. Up before the sun. Good.

She threw the covers off and padded into the kitchen for some coffee. She had a hell of a day ahead of her, and if luck had anything to do with it, she'd be on the last flight out.

Her stomach rolled with guilt as she thought about her brief encounter with Jake the night before. True to form, she'd successfully shot down any chance of *anything* between them. She didn't even give the poor guy a chance. Typical Katie, her sister would say.

She filled her coffee cup and walked to the den. First order of the day was to move all the boxes into the hallway, to make it easier to load up.

The laptop was exactly where she left it.

08AS17B61.

Reluctantly, she powered it up. The dating site popped onto the screen.

No new messages.

08AS17B61 was still offline.

She sighed and closed it. What the hell was she doing? Like McCord said, her sister's case was closed. She fell from the cliff that day. She wasn't murdered. Case closed. Right?

She felt like the walls were caving in on her. She *had* to get out of this town ASAP and back to her normal life.

Turning on her earphones to some upbeat music, she shook away thoughts of murder and sex, and got to work.

Two hours later, she bumped down the dirt road with her car packed to the ceiling with one of the last loads to the thrift store. She estimated it would take one more trip.

She picked up her cell phone and dialed the realtor that had agreed to sell the house. "Nancy, hi, it's Katie Somers."

"Hi, Katie! How are you?"

"Good, listen, any chance we can meet today?"

"We're scheduled for tomorrow… is something wrong?"

"No, I just need to get back sooner than I anticipated. For work."

"Okay, let me look through my appointments today and I'll call you back."

"Thanks, Nancy."

"No problem, will call you back."

Click.

CHAPTER 21

JAKE GLANCED AT Conroy as the two huddled around the phone in Conroy's small, cramped hotel room. It smelled like old Mexican food, cigarettes and something else that he was pretty sure was illegal. No matter how much Jake despised the guy, he was impressed that Conroy hadn't made an attempt to find another place to stay. Hell, the dumpster would have been better.

After his spat with Katie, and then hours of surveillance the night before, Jake was able to get exactly forty-five minutes of sleep before being pinged by Conroy. A conference call had been scheduled to discuss latest developments.

Mike Woodson led the call.

"Thanks to everyone for jumping on a call so quickly. Conroy, Thomas, we have some developments. Veech?"

"Thanks Agent Woodson. As you all know, along with monitoring, analyzing and decoding the three Stooges, one of my duties on this assignment is to keep an eye on local law enforcement as well. I've been monitoring daily activity as well as pulling any files on each of the Stooges. Last night, I decided to cross-reference the Stooges' fathers with the department and state files. Files for Thad Deathridge's and Kyle Howard's fathers' came up, but nothing for Scott Anderson's dad. I found that interesting, so I dug further.

I'll spare you the details on the hoops I had to jump through to find this…" he paused for applause, and when he didn't receive any, he continued, "but, buried deep inside Chief David McCord's hard drive was an encrypted file for Scott Anderson's dad. The bulk of the file was of an interview between the chief of police at the time and rookie cop McCord, twelve years ago. In the interview, McCord confesses to fatally shooting Scott Anderson's father during a routine traffic stop. However, the shooting was not justified. The subsequent paperwork goes on to conclude that Mr. Anderson had no weapon on him at the time, and although he displayed aggressive behavior, a shot wasn't warranted."

Conroy asked, "McCord was never apprehended?"

"Bingo. There are two files on the shooting, one buried in McCord's hard drive and the official one that was released. The *official* case files state that shooting was, indeed, justified. And because Mr. Anderson had a rap sheet the size of my, you know, no one questioned it. He was a thug and everyone was glad he was dead. My guess is that there was a scuffle between the two men but McCord got a little too trigger happy."

"So, McCord shot Scott's dad, and they buried the real files and that was that."

Jake blew out a breath. "Scott wants vengeance for his dad, and I'd bet McCord is his next target. Or, one of them at least."

"Exactly. And as we all know, currently, Scott and his buddies are building up to something. Also, makes me wonder, was Officer Danson killed because he was McCord's best friend? Regardless, this could be a piece of the puzzle and added reasoning why they're targeting local law enforcement."

"Amy Duncan wasn't law enforcement."

"She was having an affair with an officer. They knew her murder would directly implicate Officer Carl Winters."

"And, like Veech said, Officer Danson was McCord's buddy."

"Right."

"Has local law enforcement put it together yet?"

"By what I can tell, the three Stooges aren't on their radar at all. So, no. They're chasing their tails. But, FYI, today is the anniversary of Scott's dad's shooting."

Conroy and Jake glanced at each other. "Have there been any communications with the group today?"

"Not yet."

Jake spoke up. "Any sight of the blue sedan that left the compound the day before yesterday?"

"No."

"Not at the capitol building?"

"No."

After a moment of silence, Woodson said, "Okay gang, we know that some sort of action seems to be imminent. Conroy, Thomas, stay vigilant. Stay on it."

"Yes, sir."

Conroy clicked the phone off as Jake's gaze was drawn to the television in the corner of the room. "Turn it up."

"... *town is on edge after two back-to-back murders. Could it be a serial killer? We don't yet know, but what we do know is that we're here in front of the Berry Springs police*

*station awaiting Chief of Police David McCord, to give an
official statement on the murders..."*

Conroy raised his eyebrows and Jake had already begun
pulling his keys out of his pocket.

"How far are we from the station?"

"About six minutes."

"Let's go."

They darted out of the hotel room and into Jake's
truck. His engine roared to life as he gassed it out of the
parking lot.

Half of Berry Springs had gathered outside of the
police station, shading themselves from the blistering sun
with hats and sunglasses.

Jake slid into a parking spot a few blocks from the station and hesitated after turning off the engine. He knew he
should wait on Conroy to give instructions, but he knew
exactly what he was going to do.

Fuck it, he'll give the orders. They both stepped out of
the truck and Jake glanced toward the top of the buildings.
"I'll take eagle eye."

Conroy nodded. "I'll walk the crowd." He slid on his
earpiece and said, "Keep a cool head, Army brat."

Jake smirked as he strapped on his backpack. "Yes, sir."

Blending into the crowd, Conroy leisurely walked
down the busy sidewalk to the station. Jake detoured to the
ally between Donny's Diner and the post office, assessing
the best vantage point.

After taking a glance over his shoulder, he hopped onto
a dumpster, pulled down a metal ladder that led to the
roof, and climbed to the top of the diner.

It was at least twenty-degrees hotter on the flat, black

roof as the summer sun beat down on him. He felt his skin begin to slick with sweat as he crouched down and stepped to the edge.

"Eagle eye, on your four-thirty."

A second later, after a few crackles, he heard Conroy's voice through his earpiece. "Ten-four."

Jake set up his long-range rifle and scope and scanned the scene. Conroy blended with the crowd standing about twenty-feet from the podium. He glanced over his shoulder in Jake's direction and nodded.

From Jake's vantage point he had a clear view of the entire town square. He scanned the perimeter. Just beyond the police station was a small park flanked by a few wooded acres with tall pine and oak trees. He scanned back down to the station just as McCord made his way to the microphone.

A hush fell over the crowd.

Amy Duncan's family hovered behind him as Officer Danson's wife and child stood stoically to the side.

Jake's pulse picked up.

McCord cleared his throat. *"Good morning, everyone. As most of you know, our small town has been subjected to the horror of two murders in the last week. I want to assure you that we are doing absolutely everything we can, and exhausting every resource we have to track down the killer..."*

Jake scanned the audience. He zeroed in on a man reaching into his vest. Just cigarettes.

"... I know that everyone is on edge, and I also know that the town gossip has been rampant, so let me make one thing clear. While we are pursuing many different leads currently, we have ruled out any suspects within my office." He

glanced at Officer Carl Winters, who was in the front line of the crowd. *"We do, however, believe this is the act of a single suspect…"*

Jake widened his view and scanned the woods behind the station. He searched over the bushes and brush then slowly scanned upward.

He stopped instantly. His finger tightened around the trigger as he zoomed in.

Perched midway up a towering oak was none other than Scott Anderson, dressed in face paint and army fatigues, holding a rifle pointed directly at McCord.

"There you are," he whispered.

With laser-like focus, he zoomed in on Scott's face.

Assess, Jake. Assess. Never kill a man unless you are one hundred and ten percent sure he is a threat.

He trained, literally, years, for moments like this, and not long after he became an Army Sniper, he'd been in many life changing moments exactly like this one. He knew this. He knew how to assess his target. He knew when to shoot.

Eye locked on his target, he reached for his earpiece. "I've got Scott Anderson on your twelve-thirty, in the woods behind the station."

"On my way."

The world drowned out around him as he watched Scott's every move. Every slight move of his hands, his fingers, every twitch in his face.

He watched as Scott leaned closer to his scope.

He watched Scott's finger tighten around the trigger.

"… and while I know that many of you are living in fear right now, please know that we will find the punk who did

this. We will bring him to justice. We are the Berry Springs police force and your safety is our number one priority..."

He watched as Scott began to squeeze the trigger.

Pop!

He watched Scott tumble down the tree.

"Suspect down!" He grabbed his bag and darted down the ladder.

Jake sprinted across the street, down the block and past the police station. He spotted Conroy about halfway through the park. The crowd took notice to the two men running and began to scatter like ants. Chaos erupted.

McCord jumped from the podium, pulled his weapon and followed Jake.

Screams filled the air.

Adrenaline flooded Jake's veins as he caught up to Conroy. "To the left!" They scaled the fence and sprinted into the woods.

Not twenty-feet in, a body lay almost completely camouflaged on the ground.

Conroy knelt down and checked for a pulse. He shook his head.

"Scott Anderson."

He nodded.

"What the fuck is going on?" Chest heaving, McCord jogged up and looked down at the body.

Jake stood. "You might remember Scott Anderson... or his father, at least."

McCord's face dropped as Jake continued, "You had another split-second of life left before I took him out."

The blood drained from McCord's face as Conroy

stood. "Chief McCord, I'm going to need you to back up. This is official FBI business."

Jake's cell phone buzzed in his pocket. He glanced at the screen. Veech.

"What?"

"You and Conroy have got to get to the capitol building *now*! I think they're bombing the building today."

"You *think*?"

"Yeah, Kyle's blue sedan has been spotted entering the parking lot."

Jake looked at Conroy who was reading the same message on his cell phone. He snapped his head toward McCord. "McCord, rope this off. No one steps here, do you understand?"

McCord nodded as Jake and Conroy sprinted back to Jake's truck.

෴

"...flight two-eighty-seven confirmed, leaving Arkansas and headed to New York City at seven-thirty this evening, Miss Somers."

"Thank you, ma'am."

"Will that be all for you today?"

"Yes." Yes. That would be it. She'd be on a plane leaving Berry Springs and all the chaos with it by this evening.

Katie clicked her cell phone closed. Her fingers anxiously tapped the steering wheel as she drove down County Road 26. Although it was blazing hot, she rolled down the windows to breathe the fresh air. She needed some fresh air.

She'd just booked the last flight out of town on her way

back from dropping the last load of her sister's things at the thrift store. The house was empty. All of Jenna's things were now gone. Her stomach twisted at the thought. It was a finality that she was surprised to feel.

After her sister's death, she was in a haze for months. She worked on auto-pilot. Eventually, as more months passed she began to accept the fact that her sister was gone. But now, after cleaning out all of her things, she felt a new feeling of finality. She really was gone. She was gone forever.

And now, Katie was going to be gone, never returning to the house again. Or, hopefully, this town.

She thought of Jake.

He probably hated her now. Or did he? Maybe he didn't? Maybe she just confused the hell out of him, like she did with every guy she'd ever dated.

Contemplating, she bit her lip. Maybe she should at least apologize for her behavior the night before, for accusing him of murdering two people.

She rolled her eyes. Dammit, she sure had a way of screwing things up.

Releasing an exhale, she picked up her cell phone and dialed his number. Nerves tickled as she waited through the rings.

Voicemail.

You've reached Jake Thomas, leave a message.

"Hey Jake, it's Katie. I was just calling to say that I was…" Her attention was pulled away by a black truck hurling down the dirt road behind her. "Uh, just that I was sorry for…"

The black truck drove up on her bumper. "Oh my God," she said under her breath. She peered in the rearview mirror trying to see the driver but the windows were blacked out. The truck began flashing its lights.

Remembering she still had the cell phone to her ear, she said, "Oh, sorry, there's this black truck on my ass... flashing his lights." She began to slow down. "Anyway, I just wanted to say sorry for my behavior last night." The truck edged closer to her bumper. "Uh, I gotta go."

She clicked off the phone and tossed it in the passenger seat. "Okay, okay, dickhead. I'll pull over so you can go around."

She edged her car off the road, inches from the ditch, and slowly rolled to a stop.

To her surprise, the truck pulled behind her.

What the hell was going on? She looked around, hoping to see another car, or hell, anyone else. But they were deep in the woods and the only house for miles was hers, up ahead.

At least it was daylight. Nothing bad ever happens in broad daylight, right?

The driver's side door opened and a man she didn't recognize stepped out.

Her hand gripped the steering wheel. Should she gas it? Maybe he just needed help?

She looked over her shoulder and yelled out the window, "Something wrong?"

Before she could register what was happening, the man took two leaps and shoved his hand into her window.

A jolt of electricity paralyzed her body right before her world went black.

CHAPTER 22

JAKE'S TRUCK CLIMBED to eighty-miles per hour as they barreled down the highway. He kept both hands on the wheel as Conroy took calls from the passenger seat. The first call was to detail the events that just occurred, and other was to make a plan for the events that were about to unfold.

What seemed like an hour later, Conroy finally clicked off the phone. "Okay, we've submitted Kyle's picture to the security team at the capitol building."

"No one's seen him yet?"

"No, someone from the security team is going to walk the parking lot now to check the vehicle."

Jake tapped his thumb on the steering wheel. "Why the hell aren't we evacuating the building?"

Conroy paused before reciting a perfectly canned answer. "The intel isn't strong enough to implicate the exact target."

Jake snapped his head toward Conroy. "Bullshit!"

In a sharp tone, Conroy responded, "Keep your eyes on the road, Thomas."

Jake could feel his face heating from anger. The one thing he hated about his job in the Army was red tape. Bureaucracy. Someone making a life or death decision sitting in the comfort of their air-conditioned office. But it was the job, and he knew it. And apparently this job would be no different.

"It's up ahead."

Jake switched lanes and turned into the capitol building parking lot.

"I don't see the car."

"Me either... there's got to be side parking lots." No time to check those right now. Jake pulled into a spot closest to the main entrance and they jogged across the parking lot.

Looking straight ahead, Conroy said, "We'll monitor the building from the main security room on the second floor. The team's already been briefed. The head of security is meeting us up front."

They pushed through the front doors.

Conroy stepped forward, extending his hand, "Mr. Blidel, I'm Agent John Conroy and this is Agent Jake Thomas."

Concern and urgency reflected in Mr. Blidel's eyes as they briefly shook hands. "Pleasure to meet you both, this way please."

Jake scanned the main lobby. His eyes landed on the bathroom and he turned to his partner. "I've got to take a leak."

"What? Can't it wait?"

"I'll catch up with you guys."

As he walked across the marble floors, he dialed Veech.

"Veech here."

"You said Scott Anderson was on camera walking into the first floor bathroom a week ago, correct?"

"Yes."

"Thanks."

"Wait, what're..." But it was too late, Jake hung up.

He stepped into the bathroom, checking the stalls first. Empty. He looked around. What would Scott Anderson be doing in this bathroom for thirty-three minutes?

He checked the trashcan tops, dispensers and toilet paper holders. He was missing something. He crossed his arms over his chest and leaned against the sink.

It's always there, you just have to find it.

He looked up.

A vent.

He pushed into a stall, jumped on the toilet and hoisted himself up on the wall. After carefully sliding back the metal cover, he pulled himself up into the vent.

Dust and God knows what else stirred in the tight, dark space as he pulled his legs in.

He retrieved a flashlight from his pocket, turned it on and began to push himself further down the narrow vent. Sweat mixed with dust dripped down his face, stinging his eyes.

Inch by inch, he edged himself deeper into the vent. What was he looking for? He wasn't exactly sure, but his gut told him he was onto something. He estimated that he was almost directly above the main lobby when the light beam from his flashlight reflected off something in the center of the vent. As he edged closer, he noticed a blinking red light.

He pushed himself closer. The red light was a clock.

One minute twenty-seven seconds, twenty-six seconds….

"Oh, shit," he murmured as he reached up for his ear piece. "Conroy, can you hear me?"

Crackle, crackle, "Where the hell are you, Thomas?"

"In the vents. We've got a problem…"

"What? The vents?"

"We've got a pipe bomb, on a timer."

"A pipe bomb? You're sure?"

His breath became shallow, "Yes, sir."

"Get your ass out of there now." Conroy turned from the microphone, "Begin evacuations, immediately."

A siren began to blow as Conroy yelled, "Jake, get the hell out, now."

He was nose to nose to the device now. "There's no time. I've got to defuse it."

"That's an order Thomas!"

Chaos ensued. The sound of pounding footsteps and screams filled the air as people began to run out of the building.

Jake yanked out his earpiece and wiped the sweat from his brow.

One minute, eleven seconds…

He flexed his fingers before carefully picking up the device. He'd been through IED education and training in the Army. He knew enough to get his way around a pipe bomb but not enough to defuse it. Now was as good a time as any to learn.

Fifty-one seconds…

The screams and shouts drowned out as he tuned into his laser focus and got to work.

Thirty-two seconds…

His heart pounded wildly in his chest. Sweat ran down his face and dripped off of his the tip of his nose. He held his breath and removed the clock face.

Nineteen seconds…

Beneath the face were six black wires. He carefully turned the device over. Two cords led to the battery, one black, and one silver.

Twelve seconds. He closed his eyes and took a deep breath. *Go with your gut.*

Eight seconds.

Bracing himself, he pulled the silver wire.

With a low buzz the device went black.

He did it.

He blew out an exhale to ease his thudding heart and sat the device down. Slowly, the loud, echoing sounds from the lobby came back into focus as he reached for his earpiece.

"Jake? Jake?"

"Bomb diffused."

A moment of silence ticked by. "Leave it where it is and get down and meet me out front. SWAT's on their way."

"Yes, sir."

Jake took a moment to steady his breathing before pushing himself backwards down the vent. The screams and shouts began to dissipate as most of the building's occupants were already outside. Good.

His foot hit the vent cover and he slid out of the vent.

The building was silent now, only the low hum of chaos outside rang through the air.

He walked out of the bathroom and the hair on the back of his neck stood up. Something wasn't right.

He drew his gun, pressed his back against the wall and heard low, muffled voices somewhere across the lobby.

Yes, something was wrong.

He placed both hands on his gun and silently stepped out of the bathroom hallway. With his back to the wall, he made his way to the edge, and peered around the corner.

His breath stopped.

Standing in the far corner of the room, Kyle Howard stood behind Conroy, with one arm around his neck and a gun pointed to the agent's head.

Blood dripped from Conroy's mouth.

A hostage situation.

Jake scanned the large, open lobby. No cover what-so-ever to get any closer. He looked at the ceiling—no way to get up high for a better angle.

Shit.

"Get out your phone, now!" Kyle screamed into Conroy's ear.

Conroy slowly pulled his phone from his pocket. "What exactly do you want, Kyle?"

His voice pitched and shaking, Kyle said, "I want justice! I want my message heard!"

Not good. The guy was erratic and suicidal, which would not turn out well for Conroy, and Jake knew it. He'd seen it before.

Jake edged farther down the wall, hiding himself behind a large, potted ficus tree.

As Kyle began screaming about the injustice of "the system," Jake raised his gun. It was going to be a hell of a shot. Not only were they over a hundred feet away, Kyle had edged himself directly behind Conroy. No clear shot.

Holding his breath, Jake set his sights, narrowed his eyes and placed his finger on the trigger.

Click.

He froze. He knew that sound, the sound of a bullet sliding into the chamber.

"Drop your gun and get on your knees." The sultry female voice whispered in his ear.

Jolene Reeves.

"You don't want to do this, Miss Reeves."

"Don't tell me what I want to do, Mr. Thomas." Calm, cool and collected.

Jake's mind raced as he began to kneel down. In the distance, he heard Kyle's voice becoming more panicked.

His heart hammered. No time to make a plan. Act now.

Almost to the floor, he whipped around, knocking Jolene off her feet. Her gun fell from her hand and slid across the floor.

He dove for the gun as Jolene leapt on his back. He felt the sting of his flesh ripping underneath her nails as he reached up and flung her off his body.

He grabbed the gun, scrambled up and barreled into the lobby.

Kyle and Conroy both turned toward Jake.

Taking a step behind Conroy, Kyle yelled, "Stop! I'll shoot!" Kyle's hand tightened around the gun that was pressed against Conroy's skull.

Bolting full speed, Jake raised the gun, inhaled and...

Pop!

⋖⋗

Katie released a low groan as she rolled onto her side. She tried to open her eyes, only to realize her vision was clouded and blurry. Where the hell was she?

Hot. She was hot and sweaty and on a hard concrete floor.

Then, she remembered. The black truck, the man, the searing pain.

"Ah, waking up I see?"

The low gravelly voice sent chills up her spine. She opened her eyes again and tried to blink away the blurriness.

The figure walked up to her, his feet stopping right in front of her face. He wore dirty, green combat boots.

A popping and crackling sound came from the corner of the room and the smell of burning wood filled the air. Who the hell would have a fire in summer?

Slowly, consciousness started seeping back in and she realized she was bound. Her wrists and ankles were tied. Her pulse spiked with panic. Frantic now, she turned her head and looked up.

"Yep, you're awake." His dark, beady eyes peered down at her.

She inhaled and screamed, "Help! Somebody help me!"

Whoosh! Spots burst in her eyes as his boot slammed into her side.

He knelt down and pushed the hair out of her face. "Stay quiet. No more screaming."

She squeezed her eyes shut and pulled her knees up to her chest, writhing in pain.

"Want to know why you're here?"

Where? Where the hell was she?

He waited a moment and when she didn't answer he said, "You messaged me. This is my reply." He chuckled.

Messaged him? No. She shook her head. She'd never seen this guy before in her life.

He sat back on his heels and a smirk spread across his face. "At first I thought Jenna was reaching out to me from the dead." He laughed. "Scared the shit out of me for a second. But, it was you. I've had my eye on you since you got back in town."

Her stomach plummeted. It the guy from her sister's dating site. It was him.

"I was going to leave you alone, but, since you snooped through your sister's computer, it looks like you're starting to figure things out."

She turned her head and looked at his face. His black, beady eyes. Evil.

Was this the last face Jenna saw before she died?

Despite the pain vibrating in her side her survival instincts kicked in. *Make him talk.* She opened her mouth and with not much more than a whisper, she said, "You killed my sister."

He smiled. His thin lips curled around his brown, rotted teeth. "I guess you'll never know, will you?" He leaned closer to her. "We've got a long night ahead of us, but first things first." He rolled her to her side, grabbed the side of her shorts and yanked them down.

Terror shot through her body. No, no this can't be happening.

With her shorts pulled down mid-thigh, he stood up and walked to the corner of the room. Fear churned inside her as she waited for what was next.

Carrying a long rod, he knelt down at her backside. He took a deep breath. "This might hurt a little."

A shrilling scream burst through her vocal cords as the metal sizzled through the skin on her thigh. Pain shot like lightening through her leg; her whole body momentarily paralyzed with agony. The smell of burning flesh filled the air as he ripped the metal off of her thigh.

Chest heaving, blinded by pain, tears poured down her cheeks.

CHAPTER 23

JAKE RETURNED TO the front of the building just in time to see Kyle being rolled out on a stretcher. The SWAT team was scattered outside, scanning for more bombs.

"Jake." Conroy, whose face was streaked with dried blood, pushed away a medic who was dabbing his wounds. "You find her?"

Jake shook his head. "Nope. She must be a hell of a sprinter."

"You're sure it was Jolene Reeves?"

"One hundred percent."

"Okay, we've got men all over looking for her. We'll find her."

"So, we've got Stooge One and Two; where the hell is Stooge Three?"

"We've got Thad's picture everywhere. I sent local police to patrol the compound."

Jake nodded.

Conroy placed his hand on Jake's shoulder. "You saved hundreds of lives today… and, mine. Thank you."

"No need to thank me, it's part of the job."

"You're a hell of a shooter, Agent Thomas, and you've earned my respect."

"*Agent Conroy, we need you over here.*" Conroy smiled at Jake before turning and grouping with local police.

The scene outside was just as chaotic as inside. The security team was doing its job of keeping everyone out and away from the building. The local police had arrived and the town was in an uproar. Everyone was busy doing something.

A strong gust of wind cooled the sheen of sweat on Jake's skin and he looked up at the sky. Menacing, dark clouds floated overhead. A storm was blowing in.

His cell phone vibrated in his pocket.

Eleven messages. No shit. He quickly scrolled through and stopped on one from Katie.

"*Hey Jake, it's Katie…*" As the message went on something in his gut tickled with nerves. Something didn't sound right. Who was pulling her over in her car? He listened to it again. No, something wasn't right.

His mind raced as he dialed Veech.

"Jake, what the fuck happened? You okay?"

"Yeah, I'm fine. Hey, remember those screen names from that dating site I gave you?"

"The *dating site?* Dude you just about got blown up, why the hell are you thinking about that right now?"

"Did you uncover the identities?"

"No, man, I've been kinda busy."

Jake began walking to the parking lot. "Do it now."

"Now? What the hell is going on?"

"*Now.*"

"Alright, alright… hang on, this'll take a minute."

Jake unlocked his truck and slid behind the passenger seat. He turned the engine over.

"Almost there, hang on…"

He shoved the car in reverse and backed out of the spot.

"Okay, should be right here… hang on… okay…"

Silence.

Jake weaved through the crowd. "What?"

"*Shit*, man… 08AS17B61 is tied to Thad Deathridge. The third Stooge."

Jake hit the gas and squealed out onto the street.

"And the other screen name belongs to a Jenna Somers."

"Tell Conroy I'm headed back to Berry Springs."

Click.

Horn blaring, Jake weaved in and out of the heavy traffic until he hit the highway, where he slammed down the accelerator and dialed Katie's number.

No answer.

"Katie, its Jake, call me immediately, okay? Call me."

He drove as fast as he could and what seemed like a lifetime later, he turned onto County Road 26. The smell of rain scented the cool breeze and thunder boomed in the distance as thick clouds floated over the sun.

Lightning bolted through the sky, and he felt the electricity in the air as his truck bounced down the dirt road.

He rounded a sharp corner, his truck skidding across the gravel. Up ahead he spied her rental car on the side of the road.

His heart skittered as he pulled up behind it and jumped out of the truck.

The front door was standing open and the *ding, ding, ding,* of the keys in the ignition sounded like warning bells. Her purse and cell phone sat on the passenger seat. Not good.

He looked around. No sign of a struggle, or new dents on the car, no flat tire, nothing out of the ordinary. He grabbed her cell phone and turned it on. Six missed calls, all from him.

Where the hell was she?

He straightened, turned his face to the sky. Lightning slashed through the clouds, a cool gust of wind swept up his back.

Something was wrong.

Something was very, very wrong.

⁓

With a knife poked into her side, Thad dragged Katie out of the truck. Wind whipped through her hair as she looked around. They were out in the middle of the woods, somewhere.

"Let's go. You scream, I gut you right here." He slammed his knee into her burned thigh. Pain shot through her. She clenched her jaw and started into the woods. Her hands were tied behind her back and with every step, the fabric from her shorts rubbed against the oozing burn, causing her agonizing pain.

Dark clouds raced above her, just ahead of the rain. The storm would break loose soon. Would she be alive to see it?

She flexed her hands trying to get circulation running through her fingers and her sister's ring caught on the rope that bound her wrists together.

A fleeting moment of hope sparked.

With Thad behind her, she carefully began rubbing

the ring against the rope, over and over again, grinding the small diamonds against the fibers.

As they marched on, she began to recognize the area. They were on a secluded trail that led to the same cliff where he pushed Jenna to her death.

Each step she took led her closer to her own death.

Her heart raced with panic. She began frantically rubbing the ring against her bounds.

This can't be happening.

She closed her eyes and listened to the wind whipping through the trees, the thunder booming in the distance. His heavy footsteps behind her. She felt his hot breath panting on her neck.

Sprinkles of rain began to fall from the sky as they stepped onto the large rock.

She halted.

"Come on."

Her legs froze.

"*Come on.*" He pushed her from behind, knocking her off balance and slamming her face first into the rock. She kicked onto her back, feeling a slight pop at her wrist.

He bent over and pulled her to her feet. "Keep walking, bitch."

The clouds broke loose and rain drops began to slick the rock. She took a step, her eyes locked on the edge of the cliff, and thought of her sister. Her innocent sister, who was murdered. *Murdered.*

Rage replaced the fear and pain. She gritted her teeth, welcoming the adrenaline rush that began pumping through her veins.

She would not die. Not today.

"To the edge." He shoved the knife into her side, slicing her skin.

The pain gave her the jolt she needed. She leapt out of his grip, and using every bit of strength left in her, popped the torn rope from her wrists.

She turned on her heel—her back to the steep ravine—and lunged at her captor.

He stumbled backwards.

Thunder shook the earth as she took another leap forward, knocking the knife from his hand. They tumbled onto the rock, fists flying, legs kicking.

Scrambling to get the knife, she slipped on the wet rock, as he lept toward her. He grabbed her hair and snapped her neck back. "You bitch!" He slammed his boot into her wounded thigh. She gritted her teeth, turned and fought back. She fought like a rabid animal.

Kicking and punching, they slid closer to the edge of the rock—her back to the edge.

He released her hair and pushed up to a stance.

She looked up at him. Rain poured down his face, blood trickled down his chin. His black eyes gleamed back at her. "It's time to see your sister again."

Her heart stopped as he raised his leg.

No.

She scrambled to stand up, but before she could get her footing, the force of his boot caught her side.

Her foot slipped, her weight shifted, and with a final scream she tumbled over the edge of the cliff.

"Katie! *Katie!*" Jake burst through the tree line.

Before Thad could raise his arms to defend himself, Jake leapt across the rock and slammed his fist into his jaw. Jake jumped to the edge of the cliff as Thad's body locked up and he fell backwards, his head bouncing off of the rocks.

"*Katie!*"

He crouched down and scrambled to the edge.

"*Katie!*"

He peered over, the rain pounding down on him.

"Jake!"

With nothing but her fingertips clinging to the edge of the cliff, Katie's body dangled over the ravine, swaying in the wind.

Jake lowered down on his stomach, locked his boot in a small groove and edged his upper body off the cliff.

"Grab my hand!"

The rain poured onto her face, blinding her. "I can't! It's too slick!"

He reached farther down. "You can do it! On three!"

She blinked the rain from her eyes and felt her grip begin to waver. Gravity pulled at her dangling body like a magnet. Thunder boomed, followed by a flash of lightning in the sky.

"One!"

Her fingers began to slip.

"Two!"

A gust of wind swept across her body.

"Three!"

She kicked her legs and shot her arm up. Her hand slid into his.

He closed his grip and with one fluid movement, pulled her onto the rock.

CHAPTER 24

"BINGO." THE FOUL smell slapped him in the face as Jake propped open the metal door. He turned and yelled, "Over here!"

Brisk footsteps sounded behind him. "What you got?"

Jake angled his body so the FBI forensics team could see inside the small, dark room. "Blue barrels, all seven of them. Smells like shit."

"Peroxide. And an ass load of it."

The younger FBI team member covered his nose. "Nothing good comes out of having this much peroxide on hand."

The other snorted, "No kidding, these guys were sure as hell planning something big," he turned to Jake, "okay, we'll take it from here, thanks Thomas."

"You got it."

Jake walked across the indoor shooting range and outside into the sweltering heat.

A half a dozen unmarked vehicles scattered the front lawn of the Stooges' compound. It hadn't been fifteen hours since Jake had saved McCord's life, thwarted a bombing at the Capitol Building, and saved Katie's life, and the small town of Berry Springs was already crawling with FBI agents and journalists.

After Scott Anderson was taken to the morgue and Thad Deathridge and Kyle Howard taken into custody, the FBI forensics team had begun scouring the compound. Among an impressive collection of illegal weapons and bomb making supplies, the team uncovered blueprints for various other government facilities within the area.

The Stooges had been planning a massive, coordinated attack.

Jake shaded his eyes from the sun and felt the sweat begin to dampen his back, as he walked into the main house.

Mike Woodson glanced up, clicked off his cell phone and stepped away from Conroy.

"Thomas, I hear you just found the barrels."

"Yes, sir."

"Nice work."

They fell into step out the back door and Woodson led him to the side of the house. He paused, eyeing Jake with an expression Jake couldn't quite read.

"Well, we've had a hell of a rocky start, but I want to officially welcome you to the FBI."

Surprised, Jake raised his eyebrows.

"You saved Chief McCord's life and countless others. Not only that, it was a hell of a shot that took out Scott Anderson, and an even better shot that saved Conroy's life. You've proven yourself, son, and I'm proud I recruited you." He smiled and slapped him on the back. "So, what do you say?"

Jake smiled, "I say, Hell yeah, sir. Thank you."

Woodson nodded. "Alright, so we'll spend a few more days here and then you'll have a lot of training and work to do in D.C." He started to walk away, and then turned back. "I assume moving to D.C. isn't going to be an issue?"

Jake opened his mouth, then hesitated. He hesitated? What the fuck. This is exactly what he wanted. "Of course not sir, just tell me when and where."

"You got it."

As Woodson walked away, Jake took a deep breath. He did it. He was officially employed with the FBI. No sooner than he could exhale, Veech walked up behind him.

"Hey, man, nice work."

"Thanks."

"Woodson make it official?"

Jake nodded.

"You deserve it man." He took a swig from his water bottle. "This damn southern heat."

Jake laughed. It wasn't all that bad. "I'm gonna check out the house and will meet you outside later."

Veech flashed an okay sign as Jake sidestepped him.

The house was large, dark and messy. Bachelor pad for thugs.

After getting a few looks from the forensics team, who obviously didn't appreciate his presence while they worked, Jake made his way into the back bedrooms.

The last room down the hall was small and smelled like a musty cellar. The rebel flags that were once used to black out the sun had been pulled aside to allow for light. A layer of white dust covered most of the surfaces, presumably from the forensics team wiping for fingerprints. Jake shook his head as he looked around Thad Deathridge's room.

No family pictures, sports memorabilia, nothing that a regular twenty-something male would have in his room. No, this room was baron with just a twin-sized bed, an old television set, a PlayStation, naturally, and a tiny closet in the corner.

Clothes were haphazardly hung on hangers, but most lay crumpled on the floor. Using the toe of his boot, Jake poked around at the pile of wadded clothes on the floor.

The smell of cheap cologne mixed with body order permeated the air.

He gave the clothes one last kick then started to turn when he noticed a red, plaid shirt stuffed in the back corner of the closet.

He reached in his pocket, slid on a pair of blue latex gloves and carefully plucked it off the floor.

As the shirt uncrumpled in his hands, he noticed a small, white pearl button missing from the front.

౭

Two weeks later...

The sound of the waves washing against the shore drowned out all the chatter surrounding her.

In tactical pants, a tank top, and large straw hat, Katie hovered over what was believed to be the proximal phalanx of the fourth finger, or pinky finger. Next to that, lay a radius—lower arm—bone, almost completely intact.

"Dr. Somers, this is Dr. Shamara with forensics."

Katie pushed off the sand and wiped her palms on her pants before extending her hand.

"It's a pleasure to meet you, Dr. Shamara."

"You as well, I've read several of your articles on Native American history."

She smiled. "We're so happy you could make it on such short notice."

"Not a problem at all, this could be a huge find."

"Yes," Katie motioned to the sand, "As I mentioned on the phone, a local Anthropologist has already confirmed that these are indeed ancient human bones."

Dr. Shamara dropped to her knees and opened her bag. After pulling on latex gloves, she retrieved a magnifying glass and leaned forward.

Katie continued, "But with your expertise, I'm hoping we can be more specific."

"Hmm. Are there any more bones?"

"That's why my team is here. We're searching now."

As if on cue, Katie's partner ran up.

"Bobby, this is Dr. Shamara, archeological forensics."

Wide-eyed and hyper, he responded, "Ah, great, so nice to meet you." He turned to Katie, "Boss, I think we've got something."

Bobby led Katie to the dig site, with Dr. Shamara close on their heels.

"Here, look."

Barely visible deep in the sand lay three more bones.

Katie knelt down for a closer look. "Nice work, Bobby."

"Do you think this could be the burial site?"

"I don't like assumptions," she looked up and smiled, "but just for fun, let's assume so right now." She looked at Dr. Shamara, "Did I mention I'm glad you're here?"

"Me too." She smiled. "So, to make sure I'm on the

same page here, this could possibly be the burial site for the inhabitants of the Lost Colony?"

Katie stood. "Exactly, which would be a tremendous archeological find. As you know, this is an American mystery dating back thousands of years." She gazed at the sand. "No one's been able to determine what happened to the English settlers after they disappeared in 1587... we possibly just solved the mystery."

Bobby whimpered with excitement.

"Alright guys, we've got a lot of work ahead of us, let's move."

Hours later, Katie took a deep sip of wine and rolled her neck. The endless black ocean was highlighted by the reflection of the moon on the waves. A million stars twinkled in the night sky. The lights of a cruise ship sat on the horizon. She closed her eyes and listened to the waves lapping against the shore, as she dug her toes in the sand. It had been a long day.

It was just past ten-o'clock at night and after wrapping up a few conference calls and team meetings, she snuck out to the shore to take a moment to herself. She'd been to North Carolina before, but never on the Outer Banks. Being born and raised in Arkansas, it was always a splendid treat to be in the presence of the ocean, and Hatteras Island was beautiful, especially at night.

She heard the whistle of a nearby boat, followed with laughter and dinner party music.

A vacation. It had been so long since she'd taken a vacation. Hell, it had been so long since she'd just relaxed.

It had been two weeks since she'd left Arkansas.

After the horrific event on the mountain, Katie had

spent the rest of the day in the hospital getting poked and prodded, as well as giving statements to the police. She was also requested to give statements to a very prickly FBI agent they called Conroy.

In her interview with Conroy, she was told that Thad would be charged with attempted murder, but when she insisted that he also be convicted of her sister's murder, the conversation was shut down. Although she had turned over her sister's laptop with the incriminating messages, she got the vibe that there wasn't enough evidence, and that they had bigger fish to fry. She had little faith that justice would ever be served for her sister.

After Jake had saved her life, he tied up Thad Deathridge, who was barely conscious, threw him in the back of his truck and drove her straight to the hospital. In the chaos that followed, Jake was promptly pulled away by men in black suits. It didn't take her long to figure out that he was, indeed, an FBI Agent.

Of course, he was. She should've seen that one coming.

The very next morning, she booked the first flight out.

She hadn't heard from Jake since that day.

It was all still a blur. A dream, a nightmare.

She reached down and absent-mindedly rubbed her thigh. Even after two weeks, the burn was still tender. A constant reminder of that horrific day.

She took another sip of wine and gazed out at the ocean.

"Hi." His low, smooth voice carried through the salty air, sending her stomach sinking to her feet. She knew that voice.

She looked over her shoulder.

Jake.

She smiled. "Hi."

His face illuminated by the moonlight, he looked out at the dark ocean, then back at her. "Beautiful."

He looked different. Official. His dark hair had been cut, his face clean-shaven. He was still the rugged, sexy man that she remembered, but there was something else… authority.

She looked at the sand next to her—an unofficial invitation to sit.

He sat and said, "Congratulations on the dig."

She smiled and looked into his eyes. "Is that why you're here?"

"No."

A moment of silence slid between them.

He looked at her, with full intent behind his big, blue eyes. "I came here for two reasons. First, I wanted to be the one to tell you, face-to-face, that Thad Deathridge is not only being charged with attempted murder, but for first degree murder as well, for your sister's death."

Her mouth fell open in complete shock. Stuttering, she said, "What?… I mean, how?"

"After that day," he paused, his eyes hardened. He wasn't the only one who still wasn't over the nightmare. "My team and I searched the compound where Thad lived, and I found a shirt, missing a white, pearl button. The exact button you found at the scene."

She couldn't believe it. Tears began to wet her eyes.

"I sent the shirt to the lab, where they found remnants of blood in the fibers. I rushed the DNA testing and it was confirmed to be your sister's. And, the button places him at the scene."

She covered her mouth and gazed out at the ocean. It was as if ten thousand pounds had suddenly been lifted off of her shoulders.

"Thank you." She grabbed his arm. "Thank you, Jake."

He smiled, "It's my job."

She sniffed and almost laughed, "Yeah, about that..."

He looked down. "I couldn't tell you, I was undercover. I'm sorry." He hesitated. "I'm new at this. I'm sorry."

She smiled. She'd let that one go. "What about the other two victims? Amy Duncan, and Officer Danson?"

He glanced down at the burn on her leg and clenched his jaw. "We found the cattle prod they used to burn their victims at the compound. It's all tied together... they killed Amy and Officer Danson in retribution for Scott's father."

She shivered at hearing the words "cattle prod." "I heard about how you saved McCord's life, and hundreds of others that were in the capitol building."

He shook his head, "Not me. It was a team effort."

"Congratulations." She looked down, "So, an FBI agent."

"Yes, officially now."

A moment ticked by before she cocked her head, "What was the second reason you came here?"

He gazed at the ocean and shifted his weight, seemingly nervous all of a sudden, and she realized she'd never seen him nervous before.

His voice lowered, reflective. "I can't stop thinking about that day... about you, and if I hadn't gotten there in time."

"But you did, Jake. You saved my life. You kept me safe, just like you said you would."

He inhaled and after a moment, he looked back at her. His eyes as passionate as the night they made love under the stars.

"I just can't stop thinking about you, Katie. I... I'm in DC now, and you're in New York... I don't know how to make it work, but," he hesitated, trying to find his words, "I just know that I can't stop thinking about you."

Butterflies danced in her stomach. She smiled.

"I... don't know how to do this, I'm..."

She leaned forward and placed her hand over his. "It's okay Jake. Just kiss me."

He smiled, and underneath the twinkling stars, he leaned forward and kissed her. A long, slow, passionate kiss.

*IF YOU ENJOYED THE WOODS, CHECK
OUT THE SNEAK PEEK BELOW OF
THE NEXT BOOK IN THE SERIES!*

THE LAKE, BERRY SPRINGS BOOK #2

S HE TUGGED AT her baseball cap, pulling it just above her eyes before stepping into the dark, musty bar. Head down with her long, dark hair draped over her shoulders, she walked through the haze of cigarette smoke to the corner table in the back.

Dave's Bar was off the beaten path, and miles from a police station—a perfect place for their meeting.

The moan of old country music skipped through the rusted, red jukebox. At the bar sat two truckers with ice-cold beers, and looks that could make even the most notorious troublemaker reconsider a move. Two cowboys, complete with Wranglers and cowboy hats, played pool in the back, and a man and woman sat in the shadows up front.

She looked at the clock. Right on time.

"What can I get for ya?"

She glanced at the waitress whose gray skin told the story of two packs a day. "Shot of whiskey."

"You got it."

The front door opened. Instinctively, she slid her hand under the table and over her Glock. Her protection, her peace of mind, and her right hand. If nothing else, growing up in the slums of Chicago had taught her how to defend herself.

She locked eyes with him as he stepped through the dark bar, his hair slicked back, his coat a little too big for his small frame.

Her fingers tightened around the trigger as he slid into the seat across from her.

He grinned. "You look like shit."

"Got into a scuffle."

He shrugged and leaned back as if he had all the time in the world.

"Cut the horse shit, Chase, do you have it or not?"

He leaned forward, and in a low voice said, "I'll show you mine if you show me yours."

She stared at him, assessing. She couldn't stand the son-of-a-bitch. She released the grip on her gun and reached into her pocket and placed an envelope on the table.

He did the same.

Her pulse spiked, instinctively knowing what was next.

As he shot his hand forward grabbing both envelopes, she caught his wrist, twisted and slammed his arm on the table.

The blood ran from his face. Through his teeth, he seethed, "Let go of me, *bitch*."

She leaned forward and whispered. "I never trusted you, not for one second."

He released a muffled squeal when she broke his wrist.

"Uh, your whiskey... ma'am." Wide-eyed, the waitress set the shot on the table.

Jolene released his arm leaving him writhing in pain. She slid both envelopes in her pocket and looked up at the waitress and smiled. "Thank you, ma'am."

The waitress nodded and scurried off, obviously not unaccustomed to bones breaking in her bar.

Jolene threw back the whiskey, stood and said, "If your ass leaves that seat, I'll blow it through the wall."

His eyes spilled with rage as she smiled, laid a ten-dollar bill on the table, and after taking one last glance over her shoulder, stepped out of the bar and into the cool, crisp evening air.

ABOUT THE AUTHOR

Amanda McKinney

A life-long lover of books, Amanda McKinney wrote her debut novel *Lethal Legacy* after walking away from her career to become a stay-at-home mom. The next book in the *Berry Springs Series*, *The Lake*, will be released in the summer of 2017.

Amanda writes fast-paced novels about murder, mystery, sex and seduction, with a few laughs sprinkled in.

Visit her website at www.amandamckinneyauthor.com.

Made in the USA
Lexington, KY
16 August 2017